Zack turned to his locker. Worked the combination. Slid up the handle and popped open the door.

"Howdy, pardner!"

Zack nearly fainted. "Davy?"

"In the galdern flesh, or whatever a dang ghost is supposed to say, seein' how this ain't actually flesh hangin' off my bones no more, now, is it?"

"What are you doing here, Davy?"

"I'll make this quick. First off, don't listen to everything the Donnelly brothers might tell you. Them two still like to play with fire."

"Okay."

"Second of all, watch out for the zombie."

"The what?"

"Zombie. Corpse brought back to life but without any soul inside. Mindless and mean. Likes to rip open coffins and eat the carcasses of dead people. If he bites you while you're still alive and you somehow escape, guess what?"

"What?"

"You turn into a zombie, too!"

HAVE YOU READ
ALL OF CHRIS GRABENSTEIN'S
HAUNTED MYSTERIES?

The Crossroads
The Hanging Hill
The Smoky Corridor
The Black Heart Crypt

A

HAUNTED MYSTERY

THE SMOKY CORRIDOR

CHRIS GRABENSTEIN

A YEARLING BOOK

for R. Schuyler Hooke,
editor extraordinaire

Text copyright © 2010 by Chris Grabenstein
Cover art copyright © 2010 by Scott Altmann

All rights reserved. Published in the United States by Yearling, an imprint of Random House Children's Books, a division of Random House, Inc., New York. Originally published in hardcover in the United States by Random House Children's Books, New York, in 2010.

Yearling and the jumping horse design are registered trademarks of Random House, Inc.

Visit us on the Web! www.randomhouse.com/kids

Educators and librarians, for a variety of teaching tools, visit us at www.randomhouse.com/teachers

The Library of Congress has cataloged the hardcover edition of this work as follows:
Grabenstein, Chris.
The smoky corridor / Chris Grabenstein. — 1st ed.
p. cm.
Summary: Zack Jennings enlists his dog Zipper to try to find a lost Confederate treasure, but first they must deal with a brain-eating zombie that lives under Zack's new school.
ISBN 978-0-375-86511-4 (trade) — ISBN 978-0-375-96511-1 (lib. bdg.) —
ISBN 978-0-375-86510-7 (pbk.) — ISBN 978-0-375-89600-2 (ebook)
[1. Ghosts—Fiction. 2. Haunted places—Fiction. 3. Schools—Fiction.
4. Family life—Connecticut—Fiction. 5. Connecticut—Fiction.] I. Title.
PZ7.G7487 Smo 2010 [Fic]—dc22 2009050694

Printed in the United States of America

10 9 8 7 6 5 4 3 2

First Yearling Edition 2011

Random House Children's Books supports the
First Amendment and celebrates the right to read.

THE
SMOKY
CORRIDOR

1

The night before he officially started at his new school, Zack Jennings already had a feeling the place was haunted.

He was standing in the main hall of Horace P. Pettimore Middle School, staring at an oil painting that was staring back at him.

He stepped to his right.

The portrait's eyes followed him.

Zack moved left.

The hooded eyes followed him.

Zack hopped from foot to foot, from side to side, and the man in the portrait, some sort of Civil War soldier, kept a scornful eye on his every move.

Zack's dad came up behind him. Put a hand on Zack's shoulder. Zack stopped bouncing.

"Nervous?"

"Huh?"

"You looked jumpy. I was over there talking to Principal Smith, saw you wiggling. I figured you were either anxious about tomorrow or you were busting out some new dance moves."

Zack forced a smile.

Tomorrow. The start of a new school year. His first in North Chester, Connecticut—the small town where his father had grown up.

"I was just, you know, looking at the painting," Zack explained, gesturing at the ornately framed portrait of the Yankee soldier, whose blue uniform had a column of shiny brass buttons running up the front all the way to his bearded chin—not to mention gold ropes on both shoulders. The scowling face had, of course, stopped swinging its eyeballs back and forth the instant Zack's dad looked up at it.

"Ah! That's Captain Horace P. Pettimore. This main hall used to be the grand foyer of his mansion."

"Aha."

"He was a steamboat captain who moved here after the Civil War. Became a very wealthy, very generous gentleman farmer."

Zack knew only one farmer. A boy named Davy Wilcox. Davy wore overalls, not a Civil War uniform.

"First," Zack's dad, the history buff, went on, "Mr. Pettimore donated the property out back, several acres along the river, for the cemetery. Then, when he died, he bequeathed his mansion and all his lands surrounding it to the town, only asking that it be used for a school and that he be buried in the cemetery so he could keep an eye on the place."

Zack figured that was why they called it Horace P. Pettimore Middle School.

And why the place was haunted.

Hey, you can't build a school this close to a creepy old cemetery and not expect ghosts.

Plus, according to what Zack's dad had told him on the car ride over, the school had been the site of a "terrible tragedy" back in 1910.

"It happened in a windowless corridor in an old part of the school, the narrow hallway leading to the wood shop. A horrible fire killed Joseph and Seth Donnelly, the two boys who started it by playing with matches, and the brave teacher who tried to rescue them."

A graveyard, a terrible tragedy, two brothers and a heroic teacher killed in a corridor they couldn't escape?

Oh, yeah.

This school was definitely, one hundred percent haunted.

Zack knew a thing or two about haunted places, because he had a special gift: He could see all sorts of dearly departed souls (even the ones who popped into paintings) whom other people, especially adults like his dad, could not. He always figured it was the kind of gift that should've come with a gift receipt so he could take it back for something better, like athletic ability or super-powers.

"You ready to head on back?" Zack's dad asked. "I need to make a little speech, present the check."

"Sure."

"This way. The auditorium's in one of the modern wings, built in the seventies. The *nineteen* seventies."

They followed the flock of parents, teachers, and students

eager for the start of Pettimore's annual Back to School Night. They'd hike about a half mile back to the auditorium, where there'd be a few speeches and a couple of awards, and then everybody would have a chance to visit classrooms, meet teachers, and buy souvenir Pettimore Yankees sweatshirts and stuff. There'd probably be cupcakes, too.

As they moved with the jostling crowd, Zack once again sensed he was being watched.

He glanced over his shoulder, back at the gloomy portrait of Horace P. Pettimore.

Yep. The old guy was staring at him again.

Zack walked faster.

The two men trudged through boot-sucking mud in the dark.

Eddie was following Mr. Timothy Johnson, who, according to Eddie's boss, was the best dowser in the world. That was why Johnson was holding out a divining rod—a forked branch from a witch hazel tree.

"Find anything, sir?" Eddie asked as they made their way through the forests surrounding Pettimore Middle School.

"Silence," said Mr. Johnson. "I must remain focused."

"Yes, sir. Sorry, sir."

Now the only sound came from the chorus of crickets and cicadas chirping in the nearby meadow.

Eddie did not want to throw the little man in the bowler hat off course. Johnson was a pro when it came to finding things with his Y-shaped stick. Hidden things, like freshwater, gold mines, oil geysers, and most importantly, buried treasure.

The clues the boss had already pieced together had brought them this far, to the woods surrounding what had once been the Horace P. Pettimore estate near the town of

North Chester, Connecticut. Now Eddie was counting on Mr. Johnson to tell him exactly where to head next.

Where to dig.

"The tip!" Johnson whispered excitedly. "Look! It's bending down."

"You found it?"

"That which we seek is close at hand!"

Some unseen force yanked Mr. Johnson forward. He sailed through the brambles and branches, hanging on with all his might to the stiff twig twitching in his grip. Eddie followed.

They stumbled out of the forest into a clearing. No, it wasn't just a clearing. As they walked through the darkness across the dewy meadow, Eddie realized they had entered a cemetery.

"This way!" said Johnson, leading him through the rows of tombstones. They marched down a gently sloping lawn to the muddy edge of a river.

"This is the Pattakonck!" Eddie exclaimed. "Why, old Horace Pettimore could have sailed his steamboat straight up here from the docks down in North Chester. This is where he buried his gold! He buried it with all the dead bodies!"

"No," said Mr. Johnson, his stick now hanging limply in his hands. "The effluvia emanating from the water's surface must have overwhelmed the witch hazel."

"Say what, sir?"

"The moisture from the river temporarily threw my rod off course!"

"Oh."

The answer sorely disappointed Eddie.

"You're joshing me, right?" he said as politely as circumstances allowed.

"No. We need to start over. Perhaps we ventured too far from the school. We'll try again. . . ."

Eddie shook his head. "Nope. You, sir, are done."

"What?"

"Your services are no longer required."

"What? Don't be preposterous!"

"Excuse me." Eddie reached into his coat pocket. Pulled out his cell phone.

"What . . . what are you doing?" the dowser demanded.

"Calling my boss."

The stick quivered in Mr. Johnson's trembling hands. "Wait. As I said . . ."

"Sorry for disturbing you," Eddie said when the boss answered. "This Johnson fellow? He is absolutely worthless."

"What? How dare you!"

That was when Eddie pulled out his pistol.

"No! Don't!" Mr. Johnson pleaded. "Tell your employer that we will try again . . . tomorrow night. . . . I know I can find the hiding place. . . . I'm positive!"

Eddie cocked back the brass trigger.

Mr. Johnson quit babbling.

"So, what would you like me to do, boss?" Eddie asked.

Eddie smiled. He liked what he heard:

Do it now.

Make it look like an accident.

"And now," said Principal Scot Smith, "it gives me great pleasure to introduce George Jennings, a graduate of this school and now a partner with the New York City law firm that's been the trustee of the Pettimore estate for over a century. George?"

Zack applauded wildly like everybody else as his father made his way to the podium.

"Thank you, Principal Smith. As most of you know, Captain Horace P. Pettimore chose to retire here at the close of the Civil War because he craved the peace and tranquility of our unspoiled surroundings. He never married, never had children. So he used his vast fortune to build the Riverside War Memorial Cemetery, where veterans and paupers could be buried free of charge, and later, at his death, he left us the land and first buildings for this school."

More applause.

Zack wished his stepmom, Judy, could hear everybody clapping for his dad, but she was busy over in Chatham at the Hanging Hill Playhouse, where the musical she'd written, *Curiosity Cat*, was ending its run and attracting a lot of what they called "buzz" from producers who wanted to move the show to Broadway.

"Of course," Zack's dad continued, "if you grew up in North Chester, like I did, you also heard stories about Captain Pettimore's other fortune, his buried treasure—all the gold he supposedly stole from the Confederate Treasury." He put a hand to the side of his mouth as if he had a big secret to share. "If anyone happens to dig up a mountain of gold while you're on a nature hike out in the woods, please give me a call. That gold belongs to the Pettimore Charitable Trust!"

More laughs mingled with a few shouts of "No way, man!"

"Okay, is Tony LaGuarino here tonight?" Zack's dad scanned the auditorium.

"Over here," a gruff voice boomed.

"Come on up, Tony. I've got something for you."

Zack's dad pulled out an oversized bank check while a big man in a firefighter uniform lumbered up to the stage.

"Folks, as you know, every year, the Pettimore Trust donates a sizeable sum of money to the North Chester Volunteer Fire Department to help them teach fire safety in our schools. I remember, when I went to Pettimore Middle, we had a saying . . ."

"Don't be a Donnelly!" a parent shouted.

"Don't play with matches!" shouted another.

Zack's dad laughed. "Well, Tony, to help you guys do

the great work you do, here's ten thousand dollars for your education fund!"

The audience gave that a loud ovation.

Except for the two women seated directly behind Zack.

"Isn't the Jennings boy the one who almost burned down his house?"

"Almost burned down the whole neighborhood, I heard."

The first woman snorted. "Guess Mr. Jennings could use a little fire safety instruction in his own home."

The second woman snicked her tongue. "I hear his son is worse than the two Donnelly boys combined. A real pyromaniac."

"They're not going to let him go to school here, are they?"

"I certainly hope not."

Zack decided he needed to go to the bathroom.

Actually, he just needed to exit the auditorium.

Fast. Now. Immediately.

Head down, he worked his way out of his row.

"Excuse me," he mumbled. "Need to find the bathroom. Sorry. 'Scuse me. Bathroom."

He made his way up the aisle toward the swinging doors to the auditorium lobby. When he pushed through, he saw a pretty blond woman closing her purse.

"Hello, there," she whispered with the softest hint of a drawl. "May I help you?"

"Uh, yes, ma'am. I need to find the bathroom?"

She pointed toward the doors that led from the lobby to a corridor. "Go out the doors and take a right. Go past the gymnasium, take a left, another right, and the bathrooms are right there."

"Thanks."

"To tell the truth, I had a hard time finding them myself. This school is like a twisty ol' maze—especially since it's my first year here and all."

"Are you a teacher?" Zack asked.

The pretty lady smiled. "I sure am."

Zack smiled back.

Hey, if this nice lady is one of my teachers, he thought, *maybe school won't be so bad here after all!*

Pettimore Middle School's chief custodian, Wade Muggins, was putting in a little OT.

Overtime.

So while everybody else was all the way over on the other side of the so-called soccer green, having fun at Back to School Night in the auditorium, he was down in the cellar of the cafeteria, working late.

Earbuds stuffed in deep, he bopped into his office: the janitor's closet, in the basement of the cafeteria. Actually, "janitor's lounge" was more like it, because Wade had (without telling anyone) expanded the cramped room by busting through a wall to connect it to the root cellar of the old Pettimore mansion. He figured it might make a good rehearsal space for his rock band if he ever, you know, was in one. Nobody else knew about the root cellar. Heck, Wade only knew about it because one day, while nailing a Metallica poster to the back wall, he had accidentally swung his hammer too hard and bashed a humongous hole through the plasterboard wall.

To make certain no one ever found his secret underground Wade Cave, he had rigged up a swinging supply rack—fitted with a false back that matched the wall—to act as his private doorway. With a spring-loaded latch, all Wade had to do was lean against the third shelf, and the steel rack (fake wall and all) swung open.

He was only working late the night before school officially started to show some of what the crabby assistant principal (and royal pain in the patootie), Mr. Carl D. Crumpler, called "initiative." Wade found out from the school librarian that "initiative" meant taking charge before somebody else did. It meant stepping up to the plate and hitting a home run.

"We are under siege by an infestation of mice!" Mr. Crumpler had screamed at Wade that afternoon when a chunk of cheddar cheese had mysteriously disappeared from the faculty lounge.

It was Mr. Crumpler's cheese.

The bald-headed stooge had taped his name on it.

"Show some initiative, Mr. Muggins! Get rid of these rodents!"

For sure. He'd show old chrome dome.

Wade dragged the canister he'd taken off his barbecue grill through the secret portal and into the root cellar room. Its dirt floor rambled back about twenty feet. The only cool things in the dank place were a couple of rock star posters he'd duct taped to the walls and one of Horace P. Pettimore, who looked like he could've been a rocker. He even had the fancy soldier coat.

Wade lugged the white tank back to the spot where, earlier, he had heard mice scratching against stone.

"I'm comin' to getcha!" Wade screeched at the wall.

Then he'd pumped his fist and diddled out an air-guitar riff that would've sounded totally awesome if, you know, he'd had a real guitar and known how to play it.

There was a tiny arched hole where the fieldstone wall met the dirt floor. It looked like the entrance to a tunnel on a model-train set. Wade worked the rubber hose snaking off the gas tank into the hole.

"Time for beddy-bye, dudes!"

He twisted the valve and propane hissed through the nozzle.

Wade waited.

Ten minutes later, nothing had happened.

No mice came stumbling out of the hole, gasping for air so Wade could bop them on the head with a rubber mallet like the cats always did in cartoons.

So he figured he'd go ahead and smoke a quick cigarette.

He lit up his cancer stick and flicked the still-flaming match to the floor.

That was when the wall exploded.

5

Zack realized he must've taken a wrong turn.

In his search for the bathroom, which he really needed to use now, he had ambled up all sorts of twisty, windy hallways, some of which were modern, some old, some ancient. His new school was a dozen or more buildings all linked together by cinder block corridors lined with lockers.

He took another turn, opened a wooden door with a frosted glass panel, and found himself in an extremely narrow corridor, maybe six feet wide. The only light was the faint red glow of an exit sign reflecting off the mottled glass in the door at the far end of the hallway.

Zack could also see a classroom door on the left-hand wall and two doors close together on the right. As his eyes adjusted to the darkness, he noticed signs jutting out above the double doors: Boys, Girls.

Yes!

He had (finally) found a bathroom.

He hurried up the hallway and smelled smoke—like the wet lining of a chimney when rain trickles down it in the summer.

Then he heard a soft *boom.*

Felt the whole floor shimmy and shake.

It was pretty chilly for the first day of September, so Zack figured it was just the furnace kicking in downstairs. Nothing more. Nothing to be afraid of.

As he neared the boys' room, he could read another sign, the one hanging over the door at the far end of the hall, which was bloodred, thanks to the nearby exit sign. It said "Wood Shop."

Great.

This was *the* smoky corridor—the place where the two boys and their teacher had died.

Zack decided he really didn't need to use the bathroom after all.

He turned around and headed back the way he'd come.

He passed a porcelain drinking fountain with a steady *drip-drip-drip.*

Then he suddenly froze, because, once again, he could sense someone staring at him from behind, making him feel like he needed to defrost his neck.

Could it be the ghost of his dead mother?

That would explain the smoky smell.

His real mother had smoked so many cigarettes she'd caught cancer and died. But before she died, she summoned Zack to the railing of the hospital bed they had set up in the living room of their New York City apartment, and croaked at him, "You're the reason I smoked so much!"

"Psst!" whispered a voice behind him. "Got a match, sport?"

Zack spun around.

"How about a lighter, pal?"

It wasn't his dead mother.

The Donnelly brothers.

They had to be. One was ten, the other maybe twelve. Both were dead. Zack could tell.

Hey, he'd seen a lot of ghosts in the past three months.

Both boys had sad and sunken faces. Both were wearing tweed suit coats and ruffled bow ties. Their heavy wool pants only went down to their knees, where long, thick socks took over.

"Didn't you hear my brother's question?" asked the younger one, his voice raw and scratchy.

"You got any fire sticks on ya, pal?" asked the older one, stepping forward and shoving his little brother aside. He folded his arms across his chest and glared at Zack.

Zack coughed a little. The corridor was filled with a smoky haze.

So how did the hall become hazy all of a sudden? Zack wondered. *Is it fog rolling in from the river?*

Or had the Donnelly brothers brought the smoke from their deadly fire back with them from the grave?

And what about the heroic teacher who had died trying to rescue the two boys? Where was his ghost?

"Are you guys Joseph and Seth?" he asked. "The Donnelly brothers?"

The two ghosts nodded.

"I'm Johnny Appleseed," said the younger brother. "We need a Kit Carson."

"You ready to join up, Zack?" asked the older, tougher brother—who sort of reminded Zack of all the bullies he'd met in 2010. "Or are you some kind of lily-livered sissy boy?"

"We'll have a ton of fun, Zack!" wheezed the younger.

Zack didn't ask the ghosts how they knew his name. They just sometimes did.

"Why are you two still here?" he asked. "Why haven't you moved on from this place?"

"We're sons of Daniel Boone, boy-o," said the older brother. "This is our fort. We can't desert our post because we're not chicken like you!"

"But what about the teacher? The one who died trying to save you?"

The two boys smiled creepily as they recited a song that must've been around even in 1910.

Mine eyes have seen the glory
Of the burning of the school
We have tortured every teacher
We have broken every rule
We have marched down to the principal
To tell him he's a fool
The school is burning down.

The Donnelly brothers took one step forward. Zack took one step back.

"Well," he sputtered, "I, uh, gotta go. . . ."

Glory, glory, hallelujah
Teacher hit us with a ruler
Then he shot us in the head
To make certain we was dead
And we ain't gonna say no more, no more.

The two boys slowly vanished. So did all the smoke and the sooty smells.

Zack heard the wooden door swing open behind him.

"What in blazes do you think you are doing back here, young man?"

7

Wade Muggins was sitting on his butt in the spot where he'd landed when the wall had blown open.

Fortunately, there was no fire. Just the explosion.

And a jumble of tumbled stones.

"Far out," he muttered.

Wade had totally blown a jagged opening about four feet wide through the ancient block and mortar wall.

And off in a crooked corner, he saw one itty-bitty, teeny-weeny gray mouse.

It was chowing down on a chunk of cheddar cheese that had Assistant Principal Carl D. Crumpler's name written all over it.

8

"What's your name, young man?" the bald man snapped at Zack.

"Zack. Zack Jennings."

"Jennings?"

"Yes, sir. I'm a new student."

"Did I ask you anything about your enrollment status?"

"No, sir."

"I didn't think so."

The man had to be a teacher. He had pens and note cards stuffed in the pocket of his short-sleeved shirt. He wore old-fashioned aviator glasses, a striped tie, and a very mean look.

"You're a Jennings, eh?"

"Yes, sir."

The bald teacher, who wore his belt above his belly button, put his hands on his hips to give Zack an even sterner look.

"Any relation to George Jennings?"

"Yes, sir. He's my father."

"Humph. Figures. What, pray tell, are you doing back here in the dark?"

"I, um, got lost. Trying to find a bathroom."

"Is that so? And what do you call that room located directly behind you?"

"It's a bathroom."

"Really? I thought you said you couldn't find it?"

"Well, I did . . . eventually. . . ."

"So you were lying when you said you couldn't find the bathroom, since you obviously did!"

"Well, yeah—now I did."

"Was that lip?"

"Excuse me?"

"Were you giving me lip? Back talk? Sauce?"

"No, sir, I'm just saying . . ."

"Oh, I see. You're a smooth talker. Just like your father. Well, listen to me, buddy boy, and listen good: I will not tolerate any of your shenanigans. Is that understood?"

"Yes, sir. . . ."

"Hello, Mr. Crumpler."

It was the pretty teacher from the auditorium. She flicked on a light switch and suddenly the cramped corridor wasn't so dark anymore.

"Excuse me, young lady, who gave you permission to activate that light switch?"

The blonde laughed gently. "Well, nobody, I suppose. But I figured it didn't make much sense for the three of us to be standing here in the dark."

"Is that so? And who are you?"

The teacher held out her hand the way a princess would in a fairy tale.

"I am Daphne DuBois, Mr. Crumpler. Your new sixth-grade history teacher? We met last week during teacher orientation."

"Humph. I suppose we did." Mr. Crumpler pushed his glasses up on his nose a little.

"I do apologize that I haven't had the chance to stop by your office for a more personal introduction. I only arrived in North Chester last week, and, I confess, I've been so busy setting up my classroom and working on my lesson plans that I haven't had the chance to fraternize with my fellow faculty members."

"I am not a faculty member," said Mr. Crumpler, very deliberately. "I am your assistant principal!"

"Yes, sir, of course. And that is why I am doubly pleased to see you again."

Zack noticed that Ms. DuBois had a compassionate way of speaking, even when talking to a cranky old crab like Mr. Crumpler, who'd probably been grouchy longer than he'd been bald.

"What are you doing in this sector of the school?" Mr. Crumpler demanded.

"That," said Ms. DuBois, gesturing toward the door across the hall from the bathrooms, "is my classroom. Hopefully, several of my students and their parents will be dropping by this evening." She held up a giant cupcake carrier. "I hope three dozen will suffice." She turned to Zack. "Are you in the sixth grade this year?"

"Yes, ma'am."

"Will you be taking history?"

"I sure hope so. I mean, I think so."

"Good. It was a pleasure conversing with you again, Mr. Crumpler."

"Humph."

"Would you care for a cupcake before you go?"

"No, I would not." He pointed two fingers at his eyes, then swiveled them around to point at Zack. "I'm watching you, Mr. Jennings." He repeated the gesture. "I am watching *you*!"

Mr. Crumpler stomped away.

"Mr. Jennings?" said Ms. DuBois from the doorway. She had flicked on the lights in her classroom.

"Yes, ma'am?" Zack followed her into the room. The walls were covered with the most amazingly awesome posters and pictures. Scenes from Civil War battles. Famous faces from ancient civilizations. Drawings of the pyramids and Babylon. It was like stepping into one of his favorite video games, Age of Empires.

"Are you any relation to that handsome young lawyer who was just onstage with the firefighter?"

"He's my dad."

"Well, aren't you lucky?"

"Yeah. He's probably wondering where I am. I better go back to the auditorium."

"Would you like your cupcake now?"

Zack nodded.

"Help yourself."

Zack went to her desk and grabbed one with a whole mountain of brown frosting swirled on top. He chomped off half its head with one bite.

"Any good?" the teacher asked.

"Delicious!"

"Well, go find your father. He deserves a cupcake, too!"

"Yes, ma'am."

Zack felt so warm and happy inside he almost forgot about Mr. Crumpler and the two Donnelly brothers.

Almost.

As he headed toward the door, Zack saw an old newspaper clipping pinned to a bulletin board. The headline was huge.

TWO DONNELLY BROTHERS AND HERO TEACHER DIE IN SMOKY CORRIDOR AT SCHOOL

The corridor just outside Ms. DuBois's door.

Eddie parked his sporty convertible next to the other car.

He had the ragtop rolled up tight, because he didn't want anybody to see the dead body slumped beside him in the passenger seat.

Not that there was anybody else tooling around on this backcountry road at nine o'clock at night.

Mr. Timothy Johnson's bulging eyes looked like blood-shot hard-boiled eggs. There was a hole in the center of his forehead, where the single bullet from Eddie's pistol had entered.

Eddie stepped out onto the deserted road.

Looked both ways.

He didn't see any head- or taillights up or down the highway, so he dragged Mr. Johnson from the convertible to his own beat-up used car. He shoved the corpse behind the steering wheel.

"Enjoy the ride, sir," Eddie said as he reached across the dead man's legs to twist the key in the ignition.

The car roared to life.

Eddie adjusted the steering wheel till the nose of the vehicle was aimed at a stone wall on the other side of the road.

The Connecticut countryside was famous for its picturesque barriers made out of fieldstones stacked on top of each other. Cars were forever running off the road, slamming into them, occasionally blowing up.

Eddie jammed one end of the dead dowser's divining rod under his right knee and braced the pointy tip against the gas pedal, pressing it all the way down to the floor.

When the car burned up, so would the stick.

So would Mr. Johnson's body.

Even the lead ball in his brain would melt.

"Sir," said Eddie, "it gives me great pleasure to bid you a fond farewell."

He reached through the open window and tapped the transmission into drive.

The car blasted off.

Flew across the roadway.

Smashed into the wall.

Exploded.

Eddie's cell phone rang. He snapped it open.

"How may I be of assistance?"

It was the boss.

"Yes. Mr. Johnson just had his accident. Terrible tragedy. Where? Very well. I am on my way."

He snapped the clamshell shut.

Eddie now had to drive to a small town called Lily Dale,

New York, where, apparently, all the citizens were spiritualists, clairvoyants, or psychics.

He was to pick up a medium named Madame Marie, whom the boss had recently hired in case Mr. Timothy Johnson failed to find what they were searching for.

Eddie grinned.

If Madame Marie could not help them, he would need to locate another stone wall for her to have an accident with.

Zack found his dad in the auditorium shaking hands and laughing with old friends.

"Where'd you run off to?" his dad asked.

"Bathroom."

"Any trouble finding it?"

"A little."

Zack's dad smiled. "Don't worry. It just takes a day or two to get used to the place."

Then Zack's father gave him a guided tour of the school. "This is the gym. We'll follow this breezeway around to a bunch of interconnected classroom corridors. Right before we reach the wood shop, we'll take the exit door on the left, and that'll put us in the cafeteria, which is connected to the old Pettimore mansion—the main entrance hall."

They were basically following the same route Zack had taken earlier, so they ended up visiting Ms. DuBois's classroom, where Zack's dad had a cupcake with sprinkles and chatted with the teacher about what sort of history the sixth grade would be studying.

Meanwhile, Zack stared up at a framed print of the

Horace Pettimore oil painting he had seen hanging in the main lobby. It was displayed on the wall above the chalkboard, between prints of Abraham Lincoln and Frederick Douglass.

Fortunately, none of the famous men's eyes were staring down at Zack.

Zack wandered over to join his dad and Ms. DuBois, who looked like a model from a magazine, with golden hair shimmering down to her shoulders.

"I'm a little nervous," she said to Zack's dad, who was finishing up his cupcake. "This is my first year at Pettimore."

"I'm sure you'll do just fine."

"Thank you, Mr. Jennings. I'm certainly going to try."

"Well, we'd better take off. My wife is coming home tonight."

"Where has she been?"

"Over in Chatham. The Hanging Hill Playhouse just concluded their world premiere run of a musical based on her books."

"It's called *Curiosity Cat*," added Zack. "It might be on Broadway next!"

"Really?" gushed Ms. DuBois. "How wonderful."

"Well, it's not official," said Zack's dad. "Not yet. But there has been some very serious interest in moving the show down to New York."

He and Zack were both so proud of Judy Magruder Jennings they couldn't help bragging about her every now and then.

They were cruising down Highway 31 on their way home.

Zack's dad sighed. "Nice being back in the old building. You know, Grandpa Jim went to Pettimore when he was your age."

"Uh-huh."

"His father, too."

"Huh."

"Yep. There's a lot of ghosts walking around inside those walls."

"Ghosts?"

"You know—memories, history. Of course, when I was your age, the older kids tried to spook us, telling us stories about a crazy ghost called Scary Arie."

"Who was he?"

Zack's dad hesitated. "Nobody, really. Just a story somebody made up about a crossing guard who died saving a boy who almost got run over by a turnip truck. The truck killed Arie. Now he wanders around those twisty halls at night, looking for someone else to save. Then, of course, there's the tunnel to hell."

"The what?"

"That's what my buddy Stuart Seiden always called it. You'll see. In the winter, there's this weird strip of grass where the snow always melts. It's about six feet wide and runs from the back of the old Pettimore house all the way out to the gym."

"Dad?"

"Yeah?"

"Why doesn't Mr. Crumpler like you?"

"The assistant principal?"

"Yeah."

"I don't really remember. . . ."

"He does."

"Oh, he does, does he?"

"Yeah. He says he's gonna keep his eye on me. I think because of something you must've done."

"You met Mr. Crumpler tonight?"

Zack nodded. "When I was looking for the bathroom."

"He's been assistant principal at Pettimore for close to forty years."

"Wow. How come he never became principal?"

"I think he likes yelling at kids too much."

"So why did he yell at you?"

Zack's dad scrunched up his face. "It had something to do with Stinky."

"Who?"

"That's what we called Stuart Seiden."

"Oh."

"Okay. I remember: Mr. Crumpler accused Stinky of stealing milk cartons from the cafeteria. A whole crate of chocolate milk. So I told Stinky I'd defend him and dug up evidence that proved he was innocent."

"Cool. Your first lawyer job."

Zack's dad chuckled. "Yeah."

"So, Dad . . . do you believe in ghosts and tunnels to hell and stuff?"

Again his father hesitated. "No. Not really. They're just, you know, stories. That's all."

Right. Zack would have to tell that to the Donnelly brothers the next time he bumped into them in the smoky corridor.

11

They drove up Stonebriar Road to their brand-new
(and recently repaired) Victorian-style house.

Their home had been seriously damaged the past June
in a horrible fire. A fire started by Zack when he'd tried to
get rid of the ghost haunting a tree in the backyard.

His father had never seen that ghost and probably
wouldn't have believed in it, either.

Fortunately, his stepmother, Judy, had.

Unfortunately, Zack couldn't take his stepmom to school
with him every day to help him deal with the Donnelly
brothers, not to mention Assistant Principal Crumpler and
whatever bullies were hanging out in the halls of Horace
P. Pettimore Middle School, just waiting for a skinny kid
with glasses to show up.

Yep, starting the next day, from early in the morning
till late in the afternoon, from the first week of September
till the middle of June, Zack Jennings would have to take
care of himself.

12

The ghost of Captain Horace P. Pettimore stood over his slumbering zombie in the cavernous dining hall Pettimore had designed and had built underneath the cemetery.

"Wake," he whispered to his mindless slave. "Someone has breached the barrier. They've blasted a cannonball hole through the root cellar wall. You must stand guard. You must protect my treasure from intruders!"

The skeleton-thin zombie stirred. Opened his dull, glazed eyes.

He had been hibernating for more than two decades.

He would be hungry.

No matter. A fresh corpse had been buried in the graveyard just that morning. All the zombie needed to do was sniff it out and tear away the dirt underneath the coffin, and it would tumble down into this subterranean chamber, where the ghoulish beast could rip open the box and feast upon the rotting flesh inside.

The ghost of Horace Pettimore studied the zombie's vacant face, vaguely remembering when the creature was a man named Cyrus McNulty, a Union army soldier who had died April 9, 1864, at the battle of Deadman's Knob in Louisiana.

A few years before that fateful battle, during the Yankee blockade of New Orleans, Captain Pettimore had first learned of voodoo, a mystical religion brought to Haiti and the American South on slave ships from Africa.

It was in New Orleans that he had met a voodoo queen named LaSheena, who, for a sackful of gold coins, had taught Pettimore everything he'd needed to know to become a *bokor:* a voodoo witch doctor.

"I will give you much power, which your soul will carry in this life and into the next!" Queen LaSheena had promised.

Pettimore learned quickly. Seemed to have a natural talent for sorcery. Before long, he could do more dark deeds than even his instructor.

He could paralyze his enemies by sprinkling secret powders on the ground where they walked.

He could create undreamed-of misery by ritually damaging a voodoo doll depicting whomever he wanted to hurt.

But his greatest power was his ability to raise zombies.

To resurrect corpses.

To turn dead men into mindless slaves to do his bidding.

Using the spells taught to him by Queen LaSheena, Pettimore first sucked Cyrus McNulty's soul out of its body and sealed it in a jar—a jar still hidden in this labyrinth of tunnels beneath the school and the cemetery behind it.

Private McNulty had been buried in a mass grave along with sixty-five other dead soldiers. Captain Pettimore had resurrected them all. He'd snuck out to the burial grounds at midnight the day after they'd all died. He carried with him a list of their names and rode in a buckboard wagon filled with sixty-six empty glass jars.

First he dusted the ground with lightning powder; then he chanted the queen's mambo spells; and finally, he called the dead soldiers forth, chanting each buried soldier's name three times.

"Cyrus McNulty. Cyrus McNulty! Cyrus McNulty!"

Since McNulty, a farm boy from Indiana, had no family in Louisiana to seal up his ears with clay to make him deaf to the sorcerer's call, his wispy soul flew up through the mucky soil to be trapped as easily as a firefly in a jar. Then the lifeless body, lacking a soul and, therefore, drained of all free will, had no choice but to crawl out of his casket and dig his way back into life.

On that fateful April night, Cyrus McNulty and sixty-five other men rose from the dead to become Pettimore's army of slaves.

Yes, even after Pettimore died, McNulty, the one zombie he had kept, to act as his treasure guardian, had to obey his every command.

And what an ideal slave the living dead man was!

McNulty barely spoke. He had no desires, no ambitions, no memories or consciousness. Since he was already dead, nothing could kill him—as long as he avoided fire and no one released his soul from the jar where Pettimore had trapped it.

The resurrected McNulty was three times stronger than he had been when he was alive, making him the ideal beast of burden and protector. The zombie would fiercely guard Captain Pettimore's gold until the day when, using the darkest black magic spells ever taught him by Queen LaSheena, Horace P. Pettimore himself would rise from the dead to reclaim his treasure.

All he needed was one very special child.

The one he had been seeking for more than a century. The one he had used a voodoo charm of magic powder, herbs, dove feathers, and a pint of his own blood to attract to this place.

A blood relative.

Just one!

A new school year was about to begin, and Pettimore hoped, as he did every autumn, that the special child he sought would soon walk through the doors of Pettimore Middle School.

13

The next morning, Zack sat with Judy in the breakfast nook, swirling soggy cereal around a bowlful of milk.

Judy yawned and sipped coffee. She had gotten home very late.

"At least it's a short week," she said with a faint smile. "Just Thursday and Friday. Two days."

"Yeah," muttered Zack. His new school shirt itched at the collar. His pants were so stiff they felt like they were made out of cardboard.

Over in his dog bed, Zipper looked like Zack felt: totally bummed out because summer was officially over. His head was slumped between his paws. This was Zipper's first autumn ever. He probably sensed that something was different but couldn't figure out what it was besides the smell of dead leaves and wilted flowers. So every now and then, he exhaled a huge dramatic sigh. Zipper had lost all his zip.

"I don't know who's going to miss you more," said Judy. "Me or Zipper."

"I'm gonna miss you guys, too."

Judy reached across the countertop. Squeezed Zack's hand. He always felt better whenever she did that.

"Your dad caught the six o'clock train into the city," she said. "He said to wish you good luck and to tell you to say hi to Scary Arie for him."

"Okay."

"So who's Scary Arie?" Judy asked.

"The ghost of a crossing guard who haunts my new school."

Judy put down her mug. "You've seen another ghost?"

Zack shook his head. "Dad just told me about this dead guy, Scary Arie, who kids used to talk about back when he went to Pettimore."

"So the school isn't really haunted?"

"Well, not by a crossing guard."

"Zack? Who did you see?"

"Joseph and Seth Donnelly. The brothers who died back in 1910."

"At the school?"

"Yeah. But they also told me, 'We're sons of Daniel Boone,' which made absolutely no sense, because then they'd be the Boone brothers, right? Plus, the younger one, he said he was Johnny Appleseed and asked me to be their Kit Carson."

"Wow. Confusing."

"Yeah. Maybe they were in the drama club or something and were putting on a show for Pioneer Day and they can't move on until they complete the cast and get a kid to take the part of Kit Carson or something."

"Could be," said Judy. "How exactly did they die?"

"Well, according to Dad, they were playing with matches and started a fire. A teacher died trying to rescue them."

"How horrible. No wonder they're still haunting the hallway."

"Yeah," said Zack. "To be safe, maybe I should just skip classes for a year or two. You could homeschool me. If they want me to play Kit Carson in their show, I'd probably have to die first. . . ."

"Honey?"

"Yeah?"

"I know you don't like school, that the thought of going—"

"I'm not making this stuff up just to get out of going to school."

"I know," Judy said gently.

That made Zack feel better, because his real mother used to say that all he ever did was make up lies to get what he wanted.

"But maybe the two brothers are friendly spirits," said Judy. "Like some of the ghosts you met over in Chatham."

Grudgingly, Zack nodded. "They didn't try to spook me or anything. I think they just wanted me to play with them."

"Well, see? You haven't even started classes and you've already made two new friends."

Zack laughed. "Yeah. Two guys who've been 'held back' since 1910!"

Judy smiled. "Hey, Zack, what if things are different this year? A couple guys in the neighborhood already think you're pretty cool."

"True. But their parents don't."

"Zack?"

"Yeah?"

"Their parents won't be going to school with them."

Judy was right. Some of the guys who lived close by, like Benny and Tyler, thought it was pretty awesome how Zack and his pal Davy Wilcox had dealt with the haunted tree. A couple had even come to the Hanging Hill Playhouse to see *Curiosity Cat,* and Zack had taken them on backstage tours and introduced them to his new Hollywood movie star friends in the show.

"All I'm saying," Judy continued, "is it's a different school and you're a completely different person from who you were last school year."

Also true. Zack hadn't had a cool new stepmom last September. He hadn't even slain his first real demon until school was over and they moved up there.

He slurped down his cereal.

"Bus comes at seven-thirty," he said between soggy spoonfuls.

"You want me to walk you down the block to the bus stop?"

"Nah."

"Okay. And I promise: As soon as I get a chance, I'll head over to the library. See if Mrs. Emerson knows anything about the two Donnelly brothers."

"It's no biggie," said Zack. "I was just curious."

"So am I. And when it comes to curiosity, I wrote the book!"

Judy sipped some coffee from her mug and watched as Zack hurried down the driveway to the street, headed for his bus stop.

Zipper whined and whimpered, the way he did when he couldn't reach his favorite squishy ball under the furniture.

"I know, Zip," said Judy. "I miss him already, too."

Judy had meant to tell Zack about the obituary she had just read in the weekly newspaper. Rodman Willoughby, the eighty-something-year-old chauffeur for the late Gerda Spratling (she had been one of the human demons Zack and Judy had battled when they'd first moved to North Chester), had passed away. The newspapers called him "the Spratling family's loyal and faithful servant since 1940."

Zack had saved Mr. Willoughby's life back in June; now, just three months later, Mr. Willoughby was dead and buried.

Judy wondered if in his final days Mr. Willoughby had felt any remorse for all the horrible things the wealthy

Spratlings had ordered him to do during his years of "faithful service."

The unimaginable things he'd almost done to Zack and an innocent baby.

But Zack had saved the old geezer's life anyway. Why? "Seemed like the right thing to do at the time," he had told Judy.

Remembering that made Judy smile.

She'd been pretty lucky. Her terrific husband, George, had come with a bonus: a fantastic son, a somewhat shy boy with a big imagination and even bigger heart. Sure, he was a little skinny, wore glasses, and looked like a weakling, but Judy knew the truth: Zack Jennings was a courageous young man who wasn't afraid to do what was right or to help other people, no matter the consequences.

But he didn't need to hear about Mr. Willoughby that morning.

He had enough ghosts to deal with for one day. The two brothers, some kind of crossing guard—not to mention all the undiscovered monsters lurking in the shadows, the school bullies always looking for a skinny kid in glasses they could pick on.

Judy hoped they'd leave Zack alone.

If they didn't?

She smiled.

"You're cruisin' for a bruisin', boys."

Zack was actually feeling pretty excited as he hustled down Stonebriar Road to the corner.

Judy might be right, he thought.

Not many of the kids at Pettimore Middle School had even met Zack yet, so how could they already hate him? Especially when, like Judy had said, he was a whole new Zack.

He tugged down on the straps to his backpack. Made 'em good and snug.

Yep, this year was going to be totally different. School would be cool.

Zack let his mind wander.

A bright yellow leaf fluttered off a nearby tree and Zack imagined confetti streaming from the sky. Tons of it! A whole ticker tape parade, like when someone wins the World Series or walks on the moon.

Yep, the kids at his new school had probably heard about Zack's exploits and adventures. How, over the summer, he and his trusty dog, Zipper, had done the sort of incredibly awesome things most mere mortals and their family pets can only read about in comic books.

Zack passed a house with a Back to School banner flapping on its porch, and in his mind's eye, he could see the huge banner waiting for him at the school: WELCOME ZACK! Printed in big block letters ten feet tall. They'd probably put blinking lights in all the letters, too—like they did on Broadway.

And then a marching band would make some kind of formation around the flagpole. Maybe they'd just do a big "Z" for "Zack" and "Zipper" and leave it at that. After all, it was the first day of school and they'd only had that morning to rehearse.

Then the principal, Mr. Scot Smith, would grab the microphone and make a major announcement: Even though the school year was just beginning, Zack Jennings had already been voted Most Popular and Coolest Kid in the Sixth Grade. He'd also been elected class president. Apparently, the votes in all three instances had been unanimous.

Judy was right.

This year was definitely going to be different.

When Zack closed his eyes, he could see it all.

Then he collided with something solid and sweaty.

"Hey! Watch where you're going, wuss!"

16

Zack opened his eyes.

"I'm sorry. . . ."

He had accidentally bumped into the biggest kid waiting at the bus stop—a beefy boy with wild red hair and a sweatshirt with cut-off sleeves, the better to expose his freckled arm muscles. Three equally nasty-looking kids stood behind the giant, sniggering.

At Zack.

The neighborhood guys Zack knew, Benny and Tyler, were busy pretending they didn't know him.

"You always walk around with your eyes closed, doofus?" the redhead asked.

"No . . . I—"

"Did I say you could talk?"

"No, but—"

"There you go again. Talking without asking for permission first." He paused. Snorted some wet gunk up his nose. Stared hard at Zack. "You're the dork who lives in the dollhouse, right?"

"It's actually a Victorian but people—"

"Shuddup."

"Okay."

"You know who I am, wimp?"

Zack shook his head. "No. Sorry."

"I have a little brother. About your age."

"Uh-huh." Zack was trying not to let anybody see how much his knees wanted to knock together.

"His name is Kyle."

Uh-oh. This wasn't good.

Kyle Snertz was the bully who had picked on Zack when he'd first moved to North Chester and had kept picking on him until Zack had finally fought back and showed the world what a big baby Kyle Snertz really was.

"You're Kyle Snertz's brother?"

"That's right. Kurt Snertz. Kyle? Get over here!"

The other Snertz shuffled out of the crowd, head down. His hair was shaggy and covered his eyes.

"Yeah?" Kyle mumbled.

"Is this the punk who turned you into a crybaby?"

Kyle didn't answer. He kept contemplating his shoelaces.

"Well, little brother, don't you worry. I'm gonna make him pay."

"Okay." Kyle shuffled away.

"You see what you did to my brother, Jennings? You turned him into a wimp!"

"Well, I didn't mean to."

"Ah, tell it to somebody who cares."

"Okay." Zack could taste something metallic in his mouth. Fear.

"You ever had a toilet swirly?"

"No. Not really on my to do list. . . ."

Kurt Snertz didn't like the way he said that. He moved in closer. Clutched Zack's backpack straps.

"Well, smart mouth, now you have something to look forward to, don't you?"

Snertz dropped Zack like a sack of marshmallows.

"I'm gonna get you, you scrawny little four-eyed geek. When you least expect it, I'm gonna sneak up behind you and get you for what you did to Kyle—only what I do to you will be worse. Because when it's Snertz? It hurts!"

Early Thursday morning, Eddie drove past a sign proclaiming, "Welcome to Lily Dale: Home of the World's Largest Center for the Religion of Spiritualism."

He had driven all night to reach this far-western corner of New York State, but according to the boss, it'd be worth it: Just about every person living in the town of Lily Dale could speak to ghosts—a skill Eddie and the boss desperately required if they hoped to find Captain Pettimore's hidden gold.

Eddie parked his little car in front of a shabby cottage. The sign hanging on the lawn read "Madame Marie: Medium."

A lopsided door swung open and out waddled a bubbly woman in a bright green smock decorated with even brighter green flowers.

"Welcome," said the woman. "I am Madame Marie!"

The morning sun glinted off earrings dangling under her rosy cheeks like crystal chandeliers.

"I understand," she said mysteriously, "that you and your employer cannot find that which you seek without the aid of one who has passed over to the other side?"

"Yes, ma'am. Such is our situation."

Madame Marie toddled toward the tiny car. "It would be best if we had some object from your deceased loved one for our séance. Perhaps a favorite bit of clothing, a hat, a letter."

"We have a letter and we know where he is buried."

"Excellent! May I see the letter?" She held out her chubby hands, fingers eager to touch the past.

"I'm afraid I could not bring it with me on this trip. It is quite old, very fragile."

"Of course, of course. When was it written?"

"In 1873. Eight years after the War of Northern Aggression."

"You mean the American Civil War?"

Eddie smiled politely. "Yes, ma'am. That's what some folks call it."

18

Zack sat alone in the middle of the school bus, because Benny and Tyler were still pretending they didn't know him, and Kurt Snertz was sprawled out like a king in the back so he could keep an eye on all his terrified subjects.

"Excuse me? Is this seat taken?"

The kid sat down before Zack answered.

"Pardon me for asking, but you're new, correct?"

Zack nodded.

"I attended fifth grade at Pettimore Middle last year," the kid said, smiling from ear to ear. "So, tell me: Why does everybody already hate you? I know why they don't like me and it's not because I'm black, because, as you can see, Shareef Smith in the second row is also an African American and everybody wants to sit near him because he is cool. Me? I mostly do sudoku puzzles. Do you do sudoku?"

Zack inhaled but didn't get to answer.

"It's actually very simple. Sudoku puzzles are based on a Latin square. Do you know about Latin squares?"

Zack shook his head while his seatmate pulled two

sudoku books out of his backpack and started filling in squares on two puzzles at once—one with a pen in his right hand, one with his left.

"It's basically an $n \times n$ table filled in such a way that each symbol occurs exactly once in each row and exactly once in each column. Oh, by the way, my name's Malik. Malik Sherman."

"I'm Zack Jennings."

"Pleased to meet you, Zack. If you like, we can be friends. I promise not to ostracize you! Do you know what that word means?"

Zack nodded.

"You do?"

"Yeah. Means you've been banished."

"But did you know that 'ostracized' comes from the Greek word *'ostrakon,'* which means 'shell' or 'potsherd'?"

"No," said Zack.

"It's true! The Greeks used to write names on shells or potsherds when they were voting to kick unpopular people off their peninsula."

Zack wondered if the Greeks turned it into a TV show.

The school bus lumbered up the road. Made stops. Picked up more kids, some of whom almost sat down in the rows behind or in front of Zack before Kurt Snertz, all the way in the back, loudly cleared his throat or coughed to suggest that they'd better sit somewhere else or face his wrath.

Finally, Zack could see Pettimore Middle School.

Malik closed both sudoku books. "So, Zack, what're you doing for lunch?"

"I packed a sandwich."

"Good idea. The food in the cafeteria is rather awful. Except the chicken strips with broccoli florets on Wednesdays."

The bus chugged to a stop. The front door swung open.

Someone walking up the center aisle finger-flicked Zack on the back of the ear.

Kurt Snertz.

"See, Jennings? You just never know when I'm gonna sneak up and get you!"

The three guys behind Snertz started chuckling.

"What's the problem back there?" demanded the bus driver, watching the boys in his big rearview mirror.

"Nothin'," snorted Kurt Snertz as he and his crew moved forward.

Zack and Malik remained seated while everybody else exited the bus.

"I take it Kurt Snertz is not a fan of yours?" said Malik.

"He hates my guts."

"Excellent. He hates mine, too! See you at lunch, Zack, if not before!"

"Right."

"Promise?"

"Sure."

And to keep his promise, all Zack had to do was stay alive till lunch.

Zack studied the slip of paper one of the teachers handed him at registration and, after a few wrong turns, found his locker.

"Good morning, Zack!"

It was Ms. DuBois, the pretty teacher he'd met the night before. She was carrying a stack of books and manila folders under her chin.

"Good morning."

"All ready for a brand-new school year?"

"Yes, ma'am."

"Exciting, isn't it? I just love the smell of freshly sharpened pencils. I can't wait for the school year to start!"

Oh, yeah. Zack couldn't wait, either. School might also mean the smell of Ty-D-Bol up your nose when Kurt Snertz dunked your head in a toilet.

But he smiled at Ms. DuBois anyway. It was hard not to. She had such sky blue eyes. And that morning, she smelled like a warm cinnamon roll drizzled with icing.

"See you at third period, Zack."

"Okay!"

She bustled off around another corner.

"Hey, Zack!"

It was Benny, his so-called friend from Stonebriar Road.

"This your locker?" Benny asked.

"Yeah."

"Cool. Hey, me and Tyler meant to ask you on the bus: You gonna blow up anything here at school like you did to that tree?"

"I don't think so."

"Why not? There's a humongous old tree behind the gym building. It'd blow up real good."

"I'm not blowing up any more trees, Benny."

"I see. Movin' on to bigger stuff, huh? What? Gopher holes?"

"I don't think so."

"What? Something even bigger? Oh, man! The principal's office? That is so amazingly awesome! You'll tell us before you do it, right?"

"Sure, Benny."

"Cool!" And Benny dashed happily up the hall.

What was it Davy Wilcox used to say about Benny? *About as sharp as a bowling ball, ain't he?*

Zack smiled, remembering his first true friend in North Chester, the farm boy who didn't live in North Chester anymore.

He turned to his locker. Worked the combination. Slid up the handle and popped open the door.

"Howdy, pardner!"

Zack nearly fainted. "Davy?"

"In the galdern flesh, or whatever a dang ghost is sup-posed to say, seein' how this ain't actually flesh hangin' off my bones no more, now, is it?"

"What are you doing inside my locker?"

"Your locker? Well, dang! This used to be my locker, too!"

"What?"

"I went to school here, Zack. Back in my day, we had us this one teacher, Mrs. Crabtree—Mrs. Crabbybritches we called her—made me write 'I will not whittle in class' on the blackboard five hundred times."

"I don't believe this," Zack mumbled, practically crawling inside the locker with Davy to make sure no one passing could see him talking to an empty metal box.

"I decorated up this thing with a whole heap of magazine pictures. Snazzy cars. Bright red Ford Powermaster 861."

"What kind of car was that?"

"That one weren't no car, Zack. Powermaster's a tractor."

Davy had worked on farms all his life. First in Kentucky, which explained his funny way of talking, then right across the highway from where Zack's new house was built.

"What are you doing here, Davy?"

"Can't rightly say."

"Right. The rules."

Zack knew that ghosts weren't allowed to come and go as they pleased or to do or say whatever they wanted to do or say. Being dead was sort of like being in school.

"Can you give me a hint?"

"Why you whisperin' like that, Zack?"

"I don't want anybody to see me talking to you!"

"Don't worry, pardner. I'm invisible to everybody except you."

"Well, that just makes it worse! I look like a crazy person, sticking my head in an empty locker and talking to myself!"

"All right, I'll make this quick. First off, don't listen to everything the Donnelly brothers might tell you. Them two still like to play with fire."

"Okay."

"Second of all, watch out for the zombie."

"The what?"

"Zombie. Corpse brought back to life but without any soul inside. Mindless and mean. Can't be drowned, suffocated, shot, or poisoned. If you cut off his head, the head will stay alive and keep snappin' at ya. Fire's just about the only thing that can kill 'em."

Fire? Zack gulped. He didn't want to do that again!

"Anything else?"

"Plenty. A zombie's teeth can tear a man in half with a single bite. Likes to rip open coffins and eat the carcasses of dead people. If he bites you while you're still alive and you somehow escape, guess what?"

"What?"

"You turn into a zombie, too!"

"Gross."

"First human soul you bump into becomes your slave master."

"Yuck."

"Hang on. It gets worse. Zombies like to eat brains best of all. The younger, the better. He'll scoop out your skull, gobble 'em down, take a nap, then nibble on the rest of you for a week."

"And he's here? At the school?"

A school filled with young brains!

"Not the school but somewheres close by. Been hanging around for over a century. Just ask any of the folks buried out back in the dadgum graveyard whose bodies he ate. Now, here's the news flash: This zombie feller just woke up after snoozin' for twenty years. There could be trouble a-comin'."

"So you and your friends 'upstairs' want me to stop this demon like I stopped the others?"

"Don't know if that'll be possible this time, Zack. This here zombie is under the control of a supreme voodoo master, a ghost with juju so strong, not only can he control his meat puppet from the far side of the grave, he can also block us from seein' where the zombie's at or what he's up to."

"Juju?"

"Black magic. Witchcraft. Evil forces stronger than anything you ever gone up against. It's why you kids are gonna need guardian ghosts for a while. Can't bring no adults into this zombie situation."

"Why not?"

Davy shook his head. "They won't let me say."

"What about Judy? She's not like ordinary adults."

"Best keep her out of it, too."

"But . . ."

"Hey, Zack!"

He whipped around.

It was Malik from the bus.

"You better hurry. We don't want to be late for home-room!"

"Right. Thanks."

He waited for Malik to head up the hall, then turned around to talk to Davy some more.

Only Davy wasn't there.

20

Wade Muggins limped across the janitor's closet, pressed the third shelf on the phony supply rack, and stepped back as the secret panel swung open.

His tailbone was still aching from when he had sprained his butt during the explosion. He hobbled over to the wall and checked out the jagged hole his propane rodent repellant had blasted open.

Fortunately, nobody had heard the big kaboom, because they had all been way out back in the auditorium when it had happened. Now Wade noticed that the explosion had crackled the layer of dried hardpan coating the root cellar floor.

He kicked away some of the chunks.

"Whoa. Dude."

He dug deeper.

First he found a rusty old revolver Horace P. Pettimore must have buried in the root cellar's dirt floor. He tucked it into his pants.

Then he found a flagstone with some extremely whacked stuff carved into its top.

Wade found a whisk broom and brushed the stone clean like an umpire dusting home plate. The stone was etched with all sorts of screwy symbols like Martians probably used in their spaceship manuals; only one sentence was spelled out in earthling letters.

⌐ ∧∩⌐⅃◘⌐ ⊐>⅃⌐ษV ⌐∧ Vⅎ⅃⌐V>⅃⌐ <⌐⌐

TURN BACK NOW OR DESCEND INTO HELL

⌐⌐<V VV⌐⌐ษ <⌐Vษ⊐ ⊏◘⊏⌐ ⌐ V⌐◘⊏∩⅃ V⌐∩>⊏ษ
⌐⌐ษ ∧∩>⅃ ∩⅃∩V∩⌐∪VV V⌐⌐⊏⊏ ⌐⌐ >⅃⌐∧ ⊐∩∩ษ

"Dude, this is like a discovery on the National Geographic Channel! Totally!"

And the flagstone was right in front of the hole in the wall.

"The aliens probably left it here, man. When they hid their spaceship . . . underground!"

He studied that one line about turning back.

"Okay. On their journey, they watched a lot of our TV transmissions, *Sesame Street* and stuff, and they learned just enough English to carve that one line so they could scare people away from their parking spot!"

It made sense.

If Wade were a Martian, he would definitely hide his flying saucer where nobody could see it.

Underground. Under a school. Maybe all the way out back, under the cemetery.

And then he'd make a Martian sign so he'd remember how to find it when it was time to fly home.

Dude! This was going to make Wade so famous he would be on the local news at six *and* eleven!

He quickly ran back to his secret entrance to the Wade Cave, pulled the shelving unit shut, reset the spring, and locked himself in the root cellar. He didn't want to share his fame and glory with anyone.

"I come in peace!" he shouted into the darkness.

Then, grabbing a flashlight, he crawled into the hole he had blown through the wall.

21

fortunately, homeroom was only scheduled to last ten minutes.

Zack sat in the very last row of desks, closest to the window.

He needed to find a computer. Do an Internet search on zombies. He'd always thought they were mindless, unfeeling monsters like in those movies about the living dead. Davy made the zombie living (even though he was dead) near the school sound worse.

Zack's homeroom teacher, Mrs. Kleinknecht, was up at the front of the classroom, trying to turn on a TV monitor she couldn't reach because it was mounted to a wall bracket and she was four and a half feet tall. She dragged over an empty desk to use as a step stool and finally switched the TV on.

"Good morning, students," said the principal, Mr. Smith, whose face filled the screen. "Welcome to an exciting new year at Horace P. Pettimore Middle School!"

Yeah, Zack thought, *the resident zombie just woke up. Should make things real exciting.*

Half the kids in the room were yawning. The first day of school was always a tough one. Hard to wake up when you've gotten used to sleeping in all summer.

Zack, already bored with the morning announcements, let his eyes wander around the room. He saw Malik. Benny. Tyler.

And a girl with extremely black hair. She was slumped in her seat and carving something into the denim cover of her three-ring binder with a ballpoint pen she held like a dagger. Zack had never seen anybody with such *black* black hair. Her fingernails were painted black, too.

The girl must've sensed Zack staring at her, because she whirled around to stare back at him.

Actually, to glare at him.

While she glared, Zack noticed that her lipstick was also black and that her eyes had been circled with some kind of black gunk, which made her whole face look extremely raccoonish.

The girl shot Zack a defiant "what are you looking at, dork?" look.

Zack dropped his eyes down to his desk.

"Do you know her?" Malik whispered from his seat next to Zack's.

Zack shook his head. "No."

"Me neither. She must be new, too."

On the TV, the principal was droning on.

"It's Mexican Fiesta Day in the cafeteria. Several clubs are scheduled to hold their first meetings of the year this afternoon. The Drama Club. The Chess Club. The Competitive Math Team . . ."

Zack was totally zoning out. His eyes drifted to the window.

Where he saw another ghost.

Outside. In the parking lot. His legs inside the hood of a car.

This one was mostly a wavering silhouette against the morning sun. All Zack could make out was the slender form of a tall man wearing a chauffeur's cap.

The ghost drifted forward with a slight tremor to the rigid swing of his arms. Zack could tell that the ghost was, or had been, an old man.

He quickly glanced around the room.

The teacher was still beaming up at Principal Smith on the TV screen.

At the desks, most kids, Malik included, were obediently watching the monitor; others had their heads down, trying to catch a quick nap. Benny had a finger buried up his nose.

Zack turned back to see if the ghost had disappeared.

He hadn't.

He had marched right up to the window.

Zack recognized the ghost immediately: Mr. Rodman Willoughby, wicked Gerda Spratling's crotchety old chauffeur.

That summer, Zack had saved Mr. Willoughby's life.

Looked like it hadn't stuck.

22

After the bell finally rang, Zack headed into the hall.

Mr. Willoughby was waiting for him right outside the door.

"Hello, Zachary! I hate to trouble you, but might I have a moment of your time?"

Of course nobody else saw or heard the dead chauffeur. They didn't have Zack's "special abilities."

"Do you have math next?" asked Malik, who had come out of homeroom right behind Zack.

"Yeah."

"Me too!"

"Cool." Zack was still staring straight ahead—at the ghost of Mr. Willoughby, decked out in his chauffeur uniform and driver's cap, standing in the hallway while kids changing classes swarmed all around him. One walked straight through him and started brushing at his face like he'd just walked through a sticky spiderweb.

"Um, I need to get something out of my locker," Zack said to Malik.

"Better hurry. They only give us five minutes between

classes. And it takes three minutes and twenty-six seconds to make it to Mrs. Alessio's classroom."

"Yeah. Thanks. See you there."

Zack head-gestured to let Mr. Willoughby know which way to walk.

"Ah! A walk and talk, eh? Splendid idea, Zachary."

Zack tucked his chin down into his neck so he could talk sideways without anybody noticing.

"What happened?"

"To me? Ah, yes. It seems I died. Heart attack, I believe. I'm a bit fuzzy about the particulars. One minute I'm enjoying my microwaved dinner, and the next I'm chatting with these wise beings in white robes. Anyway, as penance for my worldly misdeeds, the judges have suggested that I perform a stint of 'community service' and kindly offered me the opportunity to become your guardian ghost."

Zack knit his eyebrows. The less he said in this extremely weird conversation with someone nobody else could see, the better.

"Ah," said Mr. Willoughby, who had apparently learned how to read minds or facial expressions since he'd passed away, "an excellent question. I'm told the position is somewhat new here at this school. And why do you need a guardian? Well, as you might've heard from Davy Wilcox—who, by the way, put in a very kind word for me upstairs—a voodoo zombie has recently awoken in his nearby hidey-hole. I know this because, well, mine was the first corpse he feasted upon when waking."

70

Zack urped. Almost tossed his cookies.

"Sorry," said Mr. Willoughby.

"I'm okay."

"Me too! Fortunately, being dead has one benefit: I didn't feel a thing while the beast ripped me apart and gobbled down my brain."

This time when he urped, Zack had to put his hand over his mouth.

"Again, my apologies," said Mr. Willoughby. "Where was I?"

"The zombie was eating your brain?"

"Ah, yes! As my spirit lingered near my corpse, I heard the zombie's master, a fiendish ghost of the worst order, state that he would soon be scouring this school for one very special child. Someone newly arrived. Fresh blood, he called it."

Zack stopped walking. "This is my first year at this school," he said. "I'm fresh blood. Do you think the zombie's master meant me?"

"I most certainly do. Oh, by the way—not a word of this to your parents. I'm told it's for their own protection."

"But . . ."

"Fear not, Zachary. You will not need your parents. You have me!"

Yeah, Zack wanted to say, *that's the scariest part of the whole deal.*

But he didn't say it.

Mr. Willoughby had just died.

He didn't want to make the poor guy feel even worse.

23

Zack hurried up the hallway—without Mr. Willoughby, thank goodness.

He had thirty seconds to make it to Mrs. Alessio's math class.

He raced around a corner, pushed open a swinging door, took a left, and nearly bumped into Mr. Crumpler, the assistant principal, who was standing in the corridor, barking into a walkie-talkie.

"Where is the janitor, Mrs. Pochinko?"

"*I don't know!*" a nasal voice shouted back.

"Find him!"

"*I'm trying!*" Mrs. Pochinko's tinny voice whined out of the radio. "*Mr. Muggins is not answering his radio.*"

"We have a serious vomitory situation in corridor twelve!"

"*I'll keep trying to locate him, sir.*"

"Hurry! It won't smell any better the longer it sits on the floor!"

"*Yes, sir.*"

Zack glanced left and saw a queasy-looking girl holding her stomach.

He wondered if the poor girl had just heard what zombies liked to eat for breakfast after they wake up from a twenty-year nap.

Mr. Crumpler saw Zack staring at the girl and the lumpy puddle on the floor.

He clipped his radio back to his belt and did that two-fingers-to-his-eyes, two-fingers-to-Zack thing again.

Zack now had two old men keeping an eye on him: one living, the other dead.

Wade Muggins was totally glad he had grabbed the flashlight before crawling through the hole in the wall.

Otherwise, he'd be stumbling around in the dark.

First he slid down some sort of angled chute and ended up on his butt again in a tunnel where the ceiling was braced with beams like you'd see in a coal mine.

"Hanging up a few lightbulbs would've been a smart move, dudes," he mumbled as he dusted himself off.

Then he remembered: Martians had burrowed this tunnel and they had X-ray vision. They didn't need light to see where they were going.

"Mr. Muggins? Where are you?"

The radio on his belt. Mrs. Pochinko. The annoying lady in the front office who talked through her nose. She worked for Assistant Principal Crumpler and was always riding Wade's butt, making him work when he'd rather be in the Wade Cave listening to heavy metal and keeping the beat on his cowbell.

"Mr. Muggins? Mr. Crumpler needs you!"

Wade unclipped the portable radio from his belt. Tossed it over his shoulder. Heard it crack open on a rock.

"Later, Mrs. Pochinko," he mumbled, and moved forward. "I'm showing some initiative down here. Making first contact with the unknown alien beings who have chosen to dig secret underground passages beneath our school buildings."

He swung his light across the mine-shaft walls. Looked back at where he had been. Just above the opening to the slanted chute, he saw another alien inscription, carved into a wooden beam.

Cool. Must be how the Martians found their way out.

Wade turned back around and kept walking forward, venturing deeper into the darkness, sloshing through puddles of stagnant water. He figured since he hadn't made any turns yet, he was basically walking out behind the old mansion, heading north toward the gym building. Maybe this was why there was always a strip of grass cutting across the snow behind the building in the winter. The heat captured in the tunnel kept the ground above it warm. He'd have to ask one of the science teachers.

No. Wait. A science teacher would want to blab to

everybody about the space creatures Wade was about to befriend, and Wade did not want to share his superstardom with any egghead science geek!

After hiking for at least as long as it takes to finger the most awesome Aerosmith guitar solo on Guitar Hero, Wade noticed that his flashlight started winking back at him. The beam was hitting dozens of tiny mirrors hanging on a wall.

He moved closer.

"Far out!"

They weren't mirrors; they were watches.

Wade counted thirty-nine antique pocket watches tacked to the wall. They seemed to be clustered in random groupings. Two watches. Three. Two.

Six rows.

Each row had a different number of pocket watches bunched together in groups. None of them had been wound lately; all the hands were frozen in place.

"Weird place to display a watch collection," Wade thought out loud.

He figured the pocket watches must've belonged to Horace P. Pettimore, the dude in the braided jacket who used to live in the old mansion before it became a school. The watches sure looked old enough to be leftovers from the Civil War. A couple had cases engraved with antique crap, like steam engines and eagles.

When Wade was a kid, his granddaddy had told him "the truth" about the whacked-out Civil War captain who had decided to build his mansion in the woods near North Chester.

"He may have been a Union soldier but he built that house with slaves. Dozens of them. He told everybody they were former soldiers but my grandpappy saw those men. Said they looked like the walking dead. Empty eyes. Glazed expressions on their faces. Took them only three years to build that house when it should've taken at least five. Then there was a big fire in the work camp and nobody saw any of those soldier boys ever again! They all died in their tents."

So, Wade thought, *if they were such speedy workers, maybe Captain Pettimore's men built this tunnel down here, too!*

But that was crazy.

Why would a Civil War captain build a coal mine under his house?

Unless all those stories he'd heard were true: Horace P. Pettimore had stolen a ton of Confederate gold. Maybe this was where he'd hid it!

Boo-yeah!

Forget the stupid Martians!

Wade was only twenty-nine but he was about to become the world's first billionaire janitor! He was going to find Captain Pettimore's gold! This was so totally awesome! He could hire Carl D. Crumpler to be his personal custodian and Mrs. Pochinko to be his maid! He could afford guitar lessons! Heck, he could afford to hire somebody good to play the guitar for him while he just strutted around the stage banging his cowbell and shaking his hair!

On each side of the wall of watches was a steep staircase leading down to . . . whatever. It was too dark to see.

The steps on both sides were made out of planks of wood that had once been painted red. A string of kerosene lanterns with red and green glass globes hung from the ceiling over each set of stairs.

But none of the lights were lit.

"I repeat: A little light down here would have been helpful, man!" Wade said to the darkness swallowing up his flashlight's dusty beam.

The gold might be down the stairs to the right, or down the stairs to the left.

Wade chose right.

Later he'd realize right had been wrong.

Very, very wrong.

25

The bell rang.

So far, Zack had survived homeroom, math, and science.

And so far, Malik Sherman had been in every one of his classes.

The girl with the black-black hair had been in Zack's second-period science class and asked a bunch of questions about death and dying and wondered if maybe the class could take a field trip to a morgue sometime to see what happens to bodies after they're dead. She seemed like a ton of fun!

Next up was history with Ms. DuBois.

"Do you like history, Zack?" Malik asked as they wormed their way through the corridors.

Zack shrugged. "Sort of. I guess. Depends."

"Well said, my friend. I, myself, wish we'd spend more time learning about the ancient history of Africa. Did you know that the Nubians, from the region we now call the Sudan, are believed to have been the first human race and that most of their customs and traditions were adopted by the ancient Egyptians?"

"No, I—"

Suddenly, Kurt Snertz, accompanied by his three buddies, was standing in front of them, blocking their path. Other kids scurried away.

"Well, if it isn't wacky Zacky and his little nerd friend Lick-Me."

"His name is Malik," said Zack. "Leave him alone."

It was barely eleven in the morning on the first day of school but Zack was already sick and tired of being pushed around by another kid named Snertz.

Kurt Snertz grabbed Zack's shirt. "What'd you just say?"

"You heard me."

"If you said what I think you said, you're dead."

Zack narrowed his eyes. "I told you to leave Malik alone."

"What? You're acting all brave because you think some teacher's gonna come along and save you?"

"No. I think you should leave Malik alone."

Snertz leaned in. "Why's that?"

"He had nothing to do with what happened between me and your little brother."

"So? Doesn't mean I can't beat him up anyway."

"Yes, it does."

"No, it doesn't."

"Does too."

"Says who?"

"Me."

"What?"

"No, I'm a 'who.'"

"Huh?"

Poor kid. Snertz wasn't used to using his brain that much at school.

Kurt tightened his grip on Zack's shirt and twisted the fabric to make the neck hole tighten up like a noose.

Choking, Zack thought about all the hours he had spent alone in his bedroom when his real mother had been alive and screaming at him from the other room. When she started yelling, Zack would slip on his headphones and watch old movies or play video games. He remembered all the action heroes he'd ever pretended to be. G.I. Joe. Indiana Jones. RoboCop.

A line from an old Clint Eastwood movie popped into his head.

"Go ahead, Snertz. Make my day."

Furious, Snertz hoisted Zack off the ground with one hand, then flung him down hard on the floor.

"Zack?" Malik said anxiously.

Zack stood up. Dusted off his pants.

"Is that it?" he asked, switching to the movie *The Incredible Hulk*. "Is that all you got?"

Snertz reared back his fist. "Why, I oughta . . ."

"Boys?"

Ms. DuBois came out of her classroom.

"What's going on out here?"

"Nothin'," snorted Snertz.

"Good! Get to your classrooms, now! Mr. Jennings? I believe you are with me for third period."

"Yes, Ms. DuBois," said Zack.

"Me too," said Malik.

"Well, hurry in, boys. The bell is about to ring!"

Ms. DuBois stepped back into her classroom as the second bell jangled loudly.

"Saved by the bell," taunted Snertz.

"You're right," said Zack, still channeling his inner action heroes. "You were."

"Come on, guys," said Snertz. "We'll take out this sack of trash later."

"Yeah! Later!" the bully pack chanted.

"*Hasta la vista,* baby," said Zack, because it was what Schwarzenegger would've said.

The bullies bounded up the hall.

"Thank you, Zack," said Malik. "By the way, exactly how many movies have you seen?"

"Too many, I guess."

"Or just enough," said Malik. "Come on! We're late!"

Malik dashed into the classroom.

Zack stood in the hallway, savoring the moment. He took in a deep breath.

The corridor outside Ms. DuBois's classroom smelled like smoke again. A wet campfire.

"You got a match, sport?"

There were the Donnelly brothers. Seth and Joseph. They'd just stepped through the boys' room door. Without opening it.

Joseph had a twisted grin on his face.

"All we need is one to have a ton of fun!"

Zack bolted into the classroom and hoped the Donnellys didn't come in after him.

Zack sat in the front row for Ms. DuBois's history class.

There was something about this teacher he really liked. She seemed to be the kind of adult who could actually become a kid's friend, the way Judy had.

Malik sat in the desk directly behind Zack, and the girl with the black-black hair was sitting in the middle of the first row, right in front of Ms. DuBois's desk.

"Good morning, everybody! Welcome to sixth-grade history. My name is Daphne DuBois and this is my first year here at Pettimore Middle School." Yep, she definitely had a Southern accent. "Is this anyone else's first year?"

Zack raised his hand. So did the girl with the raccoon eyes. Well, she kind of flopped hers up.

Ms. DuBois smiled. "Well, come on—don't be shy. Stand up and introduce yourselves." She gestured at Zack, indicating that he should go first.

So he stood.

"Um, I'm Zack Jennings. I used to live in New York City but my dad's family is originally from North Chester, so we moved back here in June."

"How wonderful! Welcome, Zack."

He sat down.

Ms. DuBois turned to the black-haired girl. "And you are?"

The girl didn't stand. "Azalea Torres," she muttered.

"Azalea. My, what an interesting name."

The girl shrugged. "Wasn't my idea."

"And when did you move to North Chester?"

"We didn't actually move here. My dad's overseas with the army. My mom wanted to be near family. Her sister lives around here. So, you know, I came with her. I kind of had to."

"Well, welcome, Azalea," said Ms. DuBois sweetly. "Okay, who here thinks history means memorizing a bunch of boring dates and the names of dead kings?"

All the kids in the classroom raised their hands, except Malik, Zack, and Azalea Torres.

"And who thinks history can be fun and rewarding?"

Azalea shot up her arm first, let it dangle in the air.

"Why do you like history so much, Azalea?"

"I guess because it's about dead people. Dead people are cool."

"Well, Azalea, I suppose you are correct. In many ways, history is, indeed, the story of those who came before us. For instance, Captain Horace P. Pettimore. The gentleman this school is named after." She gestured toward the copy of the Pettimore portrait hanging above the blackboard.

Zack wondered if there was a picture of Pettimore

hanging in every classroom. Probably. After all, it was his school.

"Who knows Captain Pettimore's history?"

Malik raised his hand.

"Mr. Sherman?"

"He came here on a paddle wheel steamboat called the *Crescent City* right after the Civil War."

"That's right," said Ms. DuBois, using a pointer to tap a picture on the bulletin board. "This was his ship. An old-fashioned steamboat like Mark Twain might've piloted on the Mississippi River. It had a big red paddle wheel in the back, two smokestacks, three decks, and a wheelhouse up top. It docked in North Chester in 1867. On board was a crew of sixty-six men, all former soldiers, who became the construction workers who built Mr. Pettimore's mansion, which, of course, is now the main entrance to our school and where Principal Smith and Assistant Principal Crumpler have their offices. Who knows why there are these lamps with red and green globes on either side of the steamboat?"

"Ooh, ooh!" Malik, of course, knew the answer.

"Malik?"

"The red lights were on the left side, and the green on the right—so at night you could tell if a boat was coming toward you or moving away. The same colored lights are on airplane wings today. Red is always on the left. Green goes on the right."

Ms. DuBois's eyes twinkled. "Is that your final answer, Mr. Sherman?"

"Yes, ma'am!"

"Well, sir, you are correct. Now then, who here has ever heard about the two Donnelly brothers?"

Everyone's hand went up.

"They died, right?" This from Azalea Torres.

"Yes, Azalea. In fact, they passed away right outside this room."

The whole classroom gasped. Except Zack.

Heck, he didn't even gasp when he *saw* the Donnellys.

"As you have undoubtedly heard, Seth and Joseph Donnelly were playing with matches in the hallway, which used to be paneled with wood. They were burning the loose-leaf pages of their notebooks, watching the hot ashes rise up and float on the swirling currents of air."

Ms. DuBois wafted her hand through the air as if it were a drifting autumn leaf. The class was mesmerized.

"Soon, the two boys started ripping pages out of their textbooks, setting those on fire, too. It wasn't long before the fire spread. First to an old corkboard filled with thumbtacked notices. Then to the wooden frame of that board. Then to the wood-paneled walls and the oil-stained floor. Fortunately, this all took place after school hours and no one else was in the building."

"Except the brave teacher," Zack mumbled.

"That's right, Zack. Mr. Patrick J. Cooper. A young mathematics instructor. This used to be *his* classroom."

Another gasp.

Ms. DuBois strolled to her desk. "He was seated right here, at his desk, working late, grading papers, when he smelled smoke." She sniffed the air dramatically. "Fearing the worst, he boldly raced out into the smoky corridor and discovered the two Donnelly brothers trying to beat down the blaze they had just ignited."

"Why didn't they just run out the fire exit doors?" asked Malik.

"Well, the exit closest to the wood shop was only put in after the tragedy, and the doors at both ends of the hallway were locked. Poor Mr. Cooper didn't have the keys."

"Who locked them?"

"The newspapers all said the Donnelly brothers did— to prevent anyone from finding out what they were up to."

"Well, why didn't they just come in here and escape out the windows?" asked Zack.

"I'm afraid they couldn't." She tapped the classroom doorknob with her pointer. "The door accidentally locked behind Mr. Cooper when he rushed into the hall to save the two orphan boys. . . ."

"Orphans?" said Azalea.

"Oh, yes. The Donnellys had no family. No father, no mother. They came here from a place called Saint Cecelia's House for Wayward Children over in Brixton. In fact, according to young Seth's diary, he considered their math teacher, Mr. Cooper, to be as close a thing to family as he and Joe had ever had."

"So how'd they die? Was it gruesome?"

Man. Azalea sure had a one-track mind.

"Well, Azalea," said Ms. DuBois, "the teacher and the two boys were trapped in that narrow, smoke-filled corridor with no exit. In mere minutes, they succumbed to what we would now call carbon monoxide poisoning. Mr. Cooper's body was found slumped in front of that doorway, the key to this classroom in his hand. All three were dead long before the fire turned that cramped corridor into a broiling hot oven that cremated their bodies. The rest, as they say, is history."

"That Mr. Cooper was a very brave man!" said a guy in the middle of the classroom.

"That he was. Which is why I am proud to say he is a distant relative of mine."

"What? Really? Wow!" The whole classroom bubbled over with excitement.

"That's awesome, Ms. DuBois," said Malik.

"Yes. It is. I am quite proud of my great-great-great-great-uncle Patrick J. Cooper."

She pointed toward a framed portrait sitting on her desk—a sepia-tone print of a man with a high forehead, beady eyes, and a bushy goatee. He looked kind of angry and, in Zack's humble opinion, not extremely heroic.

"I am even prouder to be teaching here in the same classroom where he once taught. Now then, who here besides Azalea, whose father is bravely serving overseas, has a hero hiding in the branches of their family tree?"

Most of the kids shrugged. They had no idea.

Zack figured his grandpa Jim, who had been the sheriff in North Chester years earlier, was probably pretty heroic. But he didn't want to show off.

"Well," said Ms. DuBois, "I have a feeling some of you, perhaps all of you, have incredible ancestors. That is why, this month, you will each construct your very own family trees."

"Cool. Awesome."

All of a sudden, every kid in the class *loved* history.

"All right, everybody, let's open our textbooks to chapter one. . . ."

Zack flipped his book open.

But he didn't read what was written on the page.

He had that feeling again.

Somebody was watching him.

He slowly raised his eyes.

That picture of Horace P. Pettimore hanging over the blackboard?

It was staring at him.

It was also smiling.

28

The ghost of Horace Pettimore oozed into yet another copy of his portrait and studied the children seated at their desks.

He had examined many faces this way at the start of each new school year.

He had done so for more than one hundred years.

Searching for the One. The child irresistibly lured there by his magic voodoo spell.

"This year. This year he will come."

He needed to find a child who was flesh of his flesh, blood of his blood. A relative, no matter how distant. It was why he had buried, in the front yard of his mansion, an urn filled with powders, herbs, feathers, and an incantation written in his own blood on parchment—a spell guaranteed to one day attract a family member to this place.

For Horace Pettimore needed to find a descendant in order to rise from the dead.

Yes, it could be done!

He could live forever!

He had known that orchestrating his own resurrection was possible ever since the nine-year-old girl had come to him in 1866, a year after the Civil War had ended, when he'd still lived in New Orleans. He, a Yankee carpetbagger, had just ascended to the position of supreme voodoo king after the unexpected death of Queen LaSheena.

Well, unexpected by everyone but him.

Pettimore had been plotting how to kill the old witch for months.

Anyway, that morning, he had been in the captain's quarters of his paddle wheel steamer.

The little girl gently rapped her knuckles on his door.

He immediately recognized the child as Queen LaSheena's granddaughter, the young girl he had seen playing in the back room of Queenie's voodoo shrine in the French Quarter. The girl had caramel-colored skin. Her hair was piled up high under a bright yellow head scarf, the same style her grandmother had always worn.

She had a small doll clutched in her hand.

A cloth doll dyed a deep navy blue, the color of the Union army's uniforms in the Civil War.

"Good day, Captain Pettimore," the young girl said with a sly smile. "What a pleasure it is to see you again."

Then she proceeded to tell him things only Queen LaSheena would know.

"You may think you have taken over my throne, King Pettimore," the little girl went on, "but you are sadly mistaken. For you will never have a child or a grandchild or even a niece or nephew to carry your soul forward into future generations. I have made certain of that!"

She showed him her doll.

There were pins stuck into it.

It was a voodoo doll. The little girl with the soul of Queen LaSheena dug one needle deeper into the doll's leg and the captain could've sworn he'd just been wounded by a musket ball.

"I know, for you have told me that you have no brother or sister. No cousins, aunts, or uncles." She jabbed a new needle into the doll. "You will see no children of your own." She held up the doll so he could see a likeness of his own face stitched into its head. "When you die, as all men must, your soul will find no blood of your blood nor flesh of your flesh, no earthen vessel to carry it forward. I have won. *Joc-a-mo-fee-no-ah-nah-nay,* Captain Pettimore. Enjoy your reign as the voodoo king of New Orleans. It shall be brief."

She twisted the needle in the doll's leg.

Now he could still remember the searing pain in his thigh.

But Queen LaSheena wasn't half as smart and cunning as she so arrogantly imagined.

Unbeknownst to her, there was one member of the Pettimore family he had never spoken of and, therefore, Queen LaSheena could not hex.

A beloved sister who had so disgraced the family that she'd fled Boston and disappeared. Pettimore had learned of her whereabouts, quite accidentally, from a soldier he'd met in an army hospital outside Vicksburg.

"Captain," the dying man had cried out faintly from his filthy cot, "will you kindly do me the service of informing my wife that I met an honorable end in service to my country?"

In truth, Pettimore couldn't have cared less about comforting the dying soldier's widow. He had only come to the hospital to steal antiseptics, to make certain none of his zombies infected him with diseases their corpses had carried up from the grave. But the sickly soldier, weak though he was, forced a weathered photograph with curled edges into his hand.

It was Pettimore's long-lost sister!

In the tintype, Mary was wearing a bell-skirted bridal gown and a white laurel wreath in her black hair.

"She lives with our daughter," said the dying man, mustering up just enough strength to speak, the death rattle already sounding in his chest. "In a small mill town. North Chester. Connecticut."

The soldier, of course, died.

It was fate that had decreed he should reveal what he knew about Pettimore's only family, moments before wheezing out his final breath.

So after the meeting with Queen LaSheena's granddaughter, Captain Horace P. Pettimore packed up all his belongings, his gold, and his army of zombie slaves and moved back north.

He did not find his sister or his niece.

Or any trace of them.

But he heard rumors of Mary Jane Hopkins, for that was her new name.

The bloodline lived on and he knew that despite Queen LaSheena's best efforts to thwart him, he would one day find his rightful heir.

Inspired by the pharaohs of old who had stored their treasures inside the tombs of the pyramids so they might have use of their wealth in the next life, Pettimore had his slaves construct a labyrinth of tunnels beneath his home. He created an impenetrable hiding spot for his cache of stolen Confederate gold, which would be waiting for him when he came back to life inside the body of his blood relation.

His minions, the troop of sixty-six dead Union soldiers whose souls he had stolen, used every scrap of lumber, every piece of equipment, every lamp off his old steamboat when building the captain his underground fortress.

And then he killed all the zombies.

He burned them while they slept in their tents.

All save one.

He used their deaths as an excuse to erect his war memorial cemetery, the underpinnings of which had been designed to feed fresh corpses to his one remaining zombie.

Cyrus McNulty.

The man who, without his soul, became the most ferocious beast of them all. The cemetery would give the zombie sufficient, if meager, food to tide him through the waiting.

Next, after burying the voodoo lure charm out front, Horace Pettimore generously donated his home, his land, and a substantial sum of money to the town of North Chester for the specific purpose of building a school near his burial site.

He needed children, lots and lots of children, a fresh crop every year, if he hoped to snatch the One he so desperately needed to live again.

Perhaps Pettimore would become the new boy in the front row, the skinny child with the thick glasses who kept staring back at him whenever his airy spirit slid inside a portrait.

Zack, they called him.

His family tree had deep roots in North Chester.

He might be the One.

A descendant of Mary Jane Hopkins!

Horace Pettimore could not help smiling.

Judy parked outside the North Chester Public Library, a two-story red brick building topped with a small school-house steeple.

Her good friend, the librarian, Jeanette Emerson, a feisty lady with curly white hair and bright purple reading glasses, saw her come in the front door.

"Judy! Hello, dear!"

"Hi."

Mrs. Emerson arched an eyebrow. "Did you remember to wipe your feet?"

Judy backtracked to the welcome mat. Swiped her shoes clean.

"Now then," said Mrs. Emerson, "to what do we owe the pleasure of a visit from our favorite children's author and critically acclaimed dramatist?"

"Research."

"Wonderful. You can help me reshelve these books while we chat."

Mrs. Emerson pushed a rolling cart into the stacks.

Judy dutifully followed.

"Okay, here's my question," said Judy as she slipped a neon pink murder mystery back into its proper slot on the shelf. "Actually, it's from Zack. Another paranormal research project."

"Has he seen . . . ?" Mrs. Emerson peered over the tops of her reading glasses. "An apparition?"

Judy nodded. "At the middle school."

"Oh, my."

"It was the two boys," whispered Judy. "The Donnelly brothers."

"Fascinating. What did they want?"

"For Zack to become their 'Kit Carson.'"

"I'm sorry. Their what?"

"Kit Carson. Don't ask me what it means."

"Very well. I won't."

"The older brother . . ."

"Joseph."

"Told Zack they were 'sons of Daniel Boone.' But then his little brother . . ."

"Seth."

"Said he was Johnny Appleseed."

Mrs. Emerson nodded contemplatively. "A very interesting and yet confusing family tree. Perhaps the two boys were just playing at being famous frontiersmen. It was quite the thing to do in 1910. Not that I was around back then. Almost, but not quite."

"Well, more importantly, I want to learn as much as we can about the Donnelly brothers. How exactly did they die? Was the fire their fault? Were they good kids or bad kids? Are they . . ."

"Good ghosts or bad ghosts?"

"Exactly."

"Come along," said Mrs. Emerson. "These books can wait. My curiosity, however, much like that of a certain cat I know, is demanding that I feed it some answers!"

30

It didn't take long for Judy and Mrs. Emerson to find the facts about the Donnelly brothers and the fire at Pettimore Middle School.

It was all in the *North Chester Weekly Chronicler*'s account of the terrible tragedy of Tuesday, January 11, 1910.

TWO DONNELLY BROTHERS AND HEROIC TEACHER DIE IN SMOKY CORRIDOR AT PETTIMORE SCHOOL

Joseph and Seth Donnelly, orphans, ages twelve and ten, along with their arithmetic instructor, Mr. Patrick J. Cooper, perished last night, all three having suffocated inside a cramped and smoke-filled corridor on the first floor of The Pettimore School for Children.

Mr. Cooper, the teacher, had gone into the smoky hallway in a valiant attempt to rescue his two charges who, according to firemen at the scene, had been playing with matches, attempting to ignite an "indoor campfire" with sheets of paper and wooden rulers. The fire quickly spread to a nearby bulletin board as well as the wood-paneled walls. The doorknobs at both ends of the corridor had been locked by the boys to prevent their antics being discovered.

However, Mr. Cooper, a newly arrived genteel Southerner, who had quickly established himself as a guardian to the wayward and neglected children at the Pettimore school, was grading papers in his classroom, one of two off the narrow hallway leading to the school's woodworking shop. He apparently rushed into the corridor when he smelled smoke. The door to the classroom, firemen state, "accidentally locked behind him," denying the three victims their only possible escape route, as the door to the classroom across the hall had already been locked at the close of the school day.

"The Donnelly brothers were both members of the Sons of Daniel Boone," Pettimore School Principal John Broadwater told reporters. The Boone society is the largest boys' organization in America. The group teaches camping, conservation, and outdoor pioneering skills. "I wish they had stuck to indoor games, such as treasure hunting, this winter," added Principal Broadwater.

Firefighters responding to the incident reported that the boys and their teacher were dead when they arrived on the scene. The blaze was quickly doused and contained to the one hallway.

"It was a good thing this happened after school hours," said North Chester Volunteer Fire Brigade Commander Samuel J. Morkal.

The coroner has ruled that both Donnelly boys and Mr. Cooper succumbed to smoke inhalation, having been trapped inside the corridor with the fire, which quickly consumed all the available oxygen. Their bodies were burned beyond recognition.

"Building a campfire indoors, especially in such a confined space, is never a very bright idea," Morkal said.

Patrick J. Cooper, the heroic teacher who lost his life trying to save the boys, was a recent arrival to the North Chester area.

Originally from Fort Oglethorpe, Georgia, he came to Connecticut last fall to teach mathematics and volunteered to serve as the faculty advisor for the Daniel Boone scouting group. His fellow teachers say Mr. Cooper always went out of his way to help "the weak and the orphans."

Another member of Mr. Cooper's family had also, in the past, migrated north to live in the North Chester area. In something of an ironic twist, Mr. Cooper's grandfather John Lee Cooper is buried in the "potter's field" section of the Riverside War Memorial Cemetery on the riverbank behind the school.

Funeral services for Joseph and Seth Donnelly will be held this weekend at Sacred Heart Roman Catholic Church, North Chester.

Mr. Cooper's body will be transported by railcar to Georgia for interment in the family plot.

Judy sat back in her chair and shook her head.

"How could those two boys be so stupid? An indoor campfire? They were scouts, for goodness' sake."

Mrs. Emerson nodded. "Perhaps this Sons of Daniel Boone organization no longer exists because their handbook failed to point out the obvious hazards of such foolish behavior!"

"Is that hallway still such a firetrap?"

"No, thank goodness. They rebuilt it completely. Put in a fire exit. Used brick instead of wood. Replaced one classroom, put in newfangled bathrooms—indoor plumbing being quite the rage in 1910. It's very safe back there now. Unless, of course, the two Donnelly boys turn out to be ghosts of the more dangerous sort."

"We need to dig a little deeper into this scout group," said Judy. "I'd like to find out what all that 'Kit Carson' and 'Johnny Appleseed' talk means. Why do they want Zack to join them?"

"We'll keep digging. But, Judy?"

"Yes?"

"If I were you, I'd advise Zack to steer clear of the Donnelly brothers."

"You're right. Zack doesn't need any more trouble from fires, indoors or out!"

31

Zack was starving.

He went to his locker (nobody was inside it waiting for him) to retrieve his lunch box and followed a swarm of hungry sixth graders toward the tantalizing aroma of tacos wafting up from the cafeteria's steam tables. Mexican Fiesta Day!

Girls were giggling. Guys were goofing around, slugging each other in the arms.

And Zack saw another ghost. One he recognized.

The ghost was leaning against a wall near the tray rack, wearing tights, a tunic, and a Robin Hood hat.

"What ho, Zachary!"

It was Bartholomew Buckingham, a dead actor Zack had met at the Hanging Hill Playhouse.

"How fare thee, lad?"

"Fine," Zack muttered as he bent down and pretended to tie his shoe so nobody would see him talking to a stack of plastic cafeteria trays.

"My, what a merry and motley crew is this!" said Buckingham, placing his hands on his hips and taking in the cafeteria scene. "Are these your new school chums?"

"No. Not really. It's my first day and—"

"Tut-tut. I trust you shall soon be as popular amongst your peers as I was." Buckingham struck another pose. This one involved jutting out his chin.

"Why are you here?"

"Ah! An excellent question, most excellent, indeed! I was recently anointed guardian ghost of my great-great-grandson Charles Buckingham."

The ghost gestured at a boy in the food line.

"Unfortunately, being deceased, I can do little to help the poor child. . . ." The hammy actor took off his feathered cap and held it over his heart. He sobbed some.

Zack sighed. "What do you want me to do, sir?"

"Huzzah! Glad you asked!" He sounded all bright and cheery again. "Here, then, is the situation: I fear young Charles may have inherited my heart condition—the one that did me in during my final performance as Hamlet. I'm told the critics called it 'the best death scene ever done by any Hamlet anywhere'—even if it did come one act early."

"I'm not a doctor. . . ."

"No, but perhaps you could have a word with his gym teacher? If Charles exerts himself too much, say shinnying up a rope or doing too many jumping jacks, I fear there might be complications."

"You want me to tell a gym teacher that your great-great-grandson should be excused from phys ed?"

"Huzzah! What a brilliant idea! Thank you, Zachary!" Buckingham disappeared before Zack could tell him he'd only said what he'd said so the actor could hear how ridiculous it sounded.

And then he saw something more bizarre than a swash-buckling Shakespearean actor: Malik Sherman standing on top of a chair at the far end of the dining room, flailing his arms above his head and whistling like a maniac.

32

"Over here, Zack! Over here!"

Most of the other tables were already crowded.

Malik's table, on the other hand, was almost empty. Malik sat at one end, Azalea Torres at the other. Zack went over to join them. He sat in the middle.

"So, what did you bring for lunch?" Malik asked eagerly.

"Peanut butter and jelly sandwich. It's the only thing my stepmom knows how to make."

"Well, it's an excellent choice, seeing how Pettimore Middle School has not yet been declared 'nut free.'"

Zack nodded. If ghosts like Bartholomew Buckingham kept popping in, it never would be, either.

"A bit heavy on fat content, perhaps, at eighteen grams," Malik continued, "but it will also provide sixteen percent of your daily recommended protein! To control your sugar intake, you might suggest to your mother that she use fruit preserves instead of jelly."

"She already does."

"Excellent."

"And, actually, she's my stepmother."

Azalea looked up from the book she'd been reading while nibbling nacho chips. "What happened to your real mother? Did she die?"

Zack nodded. "Yeah. Cancer."

Azalea nodded back. "Sorry."

"What's that?" Zack asked, pointing at her three-sectioned cafeteria plate. Salsa. Chips. More chips.

"My very own Mexican fiesta."

"Smart," said Zack. "I saw those tacos they were serving. They said they were beef but the meat looked kind of gray and goopy."

"Yeah," said Azalea. "They probably boiled somebody's shoe."

Zack and Malik laughed. Azalea actually smiled.

"You ever wish you could talk to her?" she asked Zack.

"Who?"

"Your mom."

Zack looked at the Goth girl. Beneath all that black makeup, she seemed pretty nice—despite how tough she pretended to be. But they'd known each other for only ten seconds. Zack hadn't even told Judy how horrible his real mother had been until they'd been together a pretty long time.

So, like he did when discussing this particular subject, he lied.

"Yeah. I wish I could talk to my mom."

"I think it'd be neat to talk to dead people," Azalea said thoughtfully.

Zack nodded. It could be. Every now and then.

"So, Zack," said Malik, "are you fascinated with the afterlife as well?"

He shrugged.

"I think it would be cool to start a séance club," said Azalea.

"Whom would you seek to converse with?" asked Malik.

"I dunno. Maybe those Donnelly brothers. I'd like to hear their side of the story."

Zack was tempted to say, *Hey, I'll give you their number.* He bit into his sandwich instead.

Benny, his friend from the neighborhood, came over to the table, holding a tray loaded down with Mexican food. Charles Buckingham was with him.

"Hey, Zack. This is my buddy Chuck. Can we sit with you guys?"

"Sure."

"Awesome!"

The two boys eagerly climbed into their seats but Benny was too excited to eat his mystery-meat taco. "Hey, Zack, I was telling Chuck about how you're going to blow up the principal's office. . . ."

"I'm not gonna blow up the principal's office, Benny!"

"Great. Because Chuck thinks maybe you should take out the cafeteria first!"

"Or the gym," said Chuck. "I hate phys ed. I'm so glad I don't have to take it until tomorrow!"

Great. Zack had one day to figure out how he could convince a gym teacher to go easy on the guy.

"So, Chuck," Zack said as casually as he could, "you ever think about seeing a cardiologist?"

"Huh?"

"You know . . . a heart doctor?"

"Can't. We don't have health insurance. I just try not to get sick."

Oh-kay. Zack needed a new idea. The direct approach wasn't going to work.

"Hello, everybody." Ms. DuBois, the history teacher, hovered near their table, holding a tray with nothing on it but a fruit cup. "I'm on cafeteria duty. Might I join you?"

"Please do, Ms. DuBois," said Malik.

And she did!

33

Wade Muggins had been wandering aimlessly through a maze of corridors underneath the school.

No.

Wait.

He'd been walking for more than an hour. He had to be beyond the school by now. Maybe underneath the woods behind the gym.

At one point, he'd dropped the rusty revolver so it would be a landmark, let him know if he was walking around in circles. He never saw the thing again.

He sniffed the air. There was a faint hint of dampness to it. Maybe he was near the Pattakonck River.

Holy crap. If he was near the river, that meant he was under the cemetery!

Dude! There were dead people snoozing in the dirt right above his head! Skeletons and worms and rotted flesh. Skulls and bones and tattered clothes.

He was about to toss his cookies.

But he had to keep going. There was gold down here, too. There had to be. Why else would somebody build a maze underground? He swung his flashlight to something painted on a row of support beams, one word on each board:

WELCOME
ABOARD
THE
CRESCENT
CITY

Freaky.

He crept up the narrow corridor.

He thought he heard breathing. Wet, wheezy breathing.

"Is anybody down here?" he shouted. "Dude? I come in peace!"

No response.

He came to a junction. Left or right? He went right again.

He shone his light into the darkness in front of him.

It flashed off two dull eyeballs.

"Whoa." Wade stepped back. The eyes looked dead. Gross. A cadaver had fallen through the ceiling when the bottom of its coffin had rotted away.

Then the eyes moved.

The two dead eyeballs weren't attached to a dead body!

Suddenly, the eyes sprang forward.

Some kind of living creature leapt into the air and sank its fangs into Wade's arm. He dropped the flashlight and screamed.

The creature released its grip and opened its jaws wide to strike again. Wade could tell by the rumble in its throat that the thing was lining up for a second lunge. He could feel and smell the monster's breath.

"No!" Wade pleaded.

Just as the beast was about to bite off his face, Wade heard an unbelievably evil voice cry out from somewhere in the darkness: "McNulty!"

The beast stopped.

"McNulty, come!"

"Yes, master," slurred a slow, dull voice.

Wade heard soft footfalls as the creature loped off into the gloom.

Wade wasn't dead! He reached for the flashlight lying on the ground. The bite in his arm hurt so bad it burned.

But he could walk. He could run!

Breathing hard, feeling woozy, he raced around blind corner after blind corner and finally stumbled into a room he hadn't been in before.

He swung the flashlight around in circles until it hit an elongated black tank with steam valves popping up at either end. Wade saw a furnace below the tank with four fuel doors. A black exhaust pipe rose out of one end, angled sharply, then disappeared through a wall like a dryer vent would. Wade, who knew a thing or two about furnaces and boilers, recognized what it was immediately: the tube boiler from an old paddle wheel steamboat.

"What's it doing way down here?" he mumbled. "The river is aboveground."

Wade needed to talk, just to hear his own voice. Ever since that thing had bit him, his head had been feeling kind of fuzzy. Fuzzier than normal.

He leaned against a neatly stacked mountain of firewood.

"Mommy? I have a boo-boo." He could feel his mind slipping away, his memories oozing out his ears.

"Twinkle, twinkle little star . . ."

Drool dribbled down his chin.

"Baa-baa black sheep . . ."

He could feel his teeth growing longer, their spiky tips pricking the lining of his cheeks.

"Ba-ba-ba-ba . . ."

He didn't recognize his own voice.

He remembered the first word he ever learned.

"Dada."

And then he could think of nothing.

Except the desire to taste human brains.

34

"Dinner will be a little late tonight," Judy said when she came up to Zack's room around six o'clock. She was carrying a brown envelope and a folded-over copy of the North Chester weekly newspaper.

"Everything okay?" Zack asked.

Zipper, who had been sleeping on his back against the baseboard, his legs sticking up in the air, rolled over to pay attention.

"Your dad's just running late at the office. I could heat something up if you're starving. . . ."

"Nah, that's okay."

"So, what're you working on?" Judy asked.

"Homework."

"On the first day of school?"

"Yeah. I'm almost done."

Judy opened up the newspaper. "Zack, there's a death notice in the obituaries I wanted you to see. . . ."

"Is it about Mr. Willoughby? Because he died a couple days ago."

"Yes. But how did you know?"

"He came to see me today."

"What?"

"At school. Davy sent him."

"Our Davy?"

"Yeah, I saw him today, too."

"At school?"

"Yeah. That place has a ton of ghosts—guess most schools do." And he hadn't even mentioned Bartholomew Buckingham.

Judy looked concerned. "Is everything okay, Zack?"

He wanted to tell her all about the zombie that Davy had warned him about. But Davy had also warned him not to tell Judy. *Can't bring no adults into this zombie situation,* he'd said. Willoughby had said basically the same thing: *Not a word of this to your parents. It's for their own protection.*

"Yeah. Everything's cool. Mr. Willoughby just wanted to say so long and Davy just wanted to say howdy. I have the same locker he had when he went to school at Pettimore."

"Well, if anything seriously spooky starts happening . . ."

"You'll be the first person I tell."

Unless Davy, Mr. Willoughby, Bartholomew Buckingham, and every other ghost I bump into at that place tells me I can't!

"You promise?"

"Yeah." Zack had never lied to Judy before. It didn't feel great. So he changed the subject.

"What's in the envelope?"

"Ah! *My* homework assignment." She opened the envelope clasp. "The Donnelly brothers belonged to a youth group called the Sons of Daniel Boone, started by Daniel Carter Beard in 1905. The sons were organized into forts."

A lightbulb went on over Zack's head (or it would've if he were a cartoon): "That's why they said the school was their fort!"

"Exactly. And the officers of the fort took on the names of famous frontiersmen, like Daniel Boone, Johnny Appleseed . . ."

"And Kit Carson!"

Judy nodded. "The sons did all sorts of activities. They'd have treasure hunts, study nature, go camping. . . ."

Judy's voice trailed off.

"What?"

"Well, Zack, for some strange reason, the Donnelly brothers decided to build an indoor campfire in that back corridor where you saw them."

"You're kidding."

"Nope. If I were you, I'd steer clear of Seth and Joseph Donnelly. I think they're, you know, troublemakers."

"Davy kind of said the same thing. He told me they still liked to play with fire."

Zack, on the other hand, never wanted to mess with it again!

35

Wade the Zombie stared at the ghostly boy standing in front of him, the first human soul he had encountered since the beast had sprung out of the darkness and bit him.

"Who are you?" the ghost boy asked.

"Ah boo blot blow, blasder," Wade grunted in reply.

"Huh?"

"I do not know, master," Wade grunted more clearly.

That made the ghost boy smile.

"Did you just call me master?"

"Yes, master."

A second ghost boy drifted into the room. Instinctively, Wade jumped forward to put his body between this new boy and his master.

"Must protect master!"

The new boy laughed. "What did that drool bucket just say?"

"He said he had to protect me because I'm his master."

"Seth? What's going on here, little brother?"

"Well, Joseph, I found this feller stumbling around down here in the dark."

"You think he's a . . . ?"

"Sure looks like one."

"Mush problect blasder," Wade grumbled.

"Sure sounds like one, too!"

The boys turned to face him again.

The older one spoke: "Not for nothin', pal, but were you recently bitten by a zombie?"

Wade turned to the younger one.

"You may answer," said the master.

"Yes, master. Yes. I was bitten."

"And you escaped before he could crack open your skull and scoop out your brains?"

"Yes."

The two boys both looked very pleased with his answers, the younger one more than the older.

"Hot diggity dog, Joe, he's callin' me master!"

"That means he's your zombie slave, Seth!" said the older boy. "We can make him do all the stuff we can't do no more! We can finally get this show on the road!"

The ghost boys moved closer.

"Hop on your left foot!" snapped the younger one, the boy called Seth.

Wade hopped.

"Pick up some firewood and drop it on your toe."

Wade did that, too. It did not hurt.

"Say, Zombie Man," asked the older boy, "do you know how to operate a furnace?"

"Yes."

"You packin' any matches?"

The zombie reached into his pants. Showed the ghost boys the box of wooden matches the man he used to be always carried in his pants pockets to light his smokes and pick his teeth.

"Hot diggity dog!" said Seth.

Then he and his brother started singing.

Mine eyes have seen the glory
Of the burning of the school . . .

36

That night, Eddie and Madame Marie snuck into the cemetery behind the school.

They had driven straight from Lily Dale, New York, to North Chester, Connecticut. Eddie led the way through the iron graveyard gates. Madame Marie carried a worn leather briefcase. In it were all the tools she would need to conduct a séance.

"Where are the physical remains of the spirit you wish to contact?" she asked Eddie as she adjusted her turban.

"Over yonder, ma'am."

They hiked downhill toward the Pattakonck River, which flowed through the darkness like a velvet ribbon. Madame Marie swung her flashlight beam back and forth across the rows of weathered headstones. It hit upon one, the largest marker in the cemetery.

"Ma'am?" said Eddie. "That isn't the spirit we wish to contact."

"This Captain Pettimore must have been a Mason. See that carving at the top of his stone?"

Madame Marie pointed at the image of an eye inside a

triangle surrounded by sunbeams. It reminded Eddie of the floating eyeball over the pyramid on the back of a one-dollar bill.

"Masons call that the Eye of Providence. It serves as a constant reminder that a Mason's deeds are always being observed by the Grand Architect of the Universe!"

"Fascinating," said Eddie, who figured he might as well see if the medium could discern anything else about the plundering Yankee gold thief. "What else can you tell me after studying that stone?"

Madame Marie focused her flashlight beam on the tall slab of marble.

CAPTAIN HORACE PHINEAS PETTIMORE
1825–1900

ALL THAT I HAVE
I LEAVE FOR HE
WHO COMES AFTER ME

"Only that it is a lovely piece of chisel work—I love the delicate, lacy framing above and below the epitaph—and that Captain Pettimore must have been a very generous soul, leaving all that he had to those who came after him. Quite impressive."

Yes, ma'am, Eddie thought, *it's easy to give money away when it isn't your own.*

"Now," warbled Madame Marie, "where is the soul you wish me to contact?"

"This way, ma'am."

Crickets chirped. Frogs croaked. They hiked downhill.

"Our man is buried way down there," said Eddie, pointing toward a clump of short stones near the river-bank. "They put him in with the paupers—poor folks buried free of charge."

They came to the smallest of the small headstones.

Madame Marie read the words chiseled into the tiny slab:

JOHN LEE COOPER
1835–1873
CSA
HOORAY, MY BRAVE BOYS,
LET'S REJOICE AT HIS FALL.
FOR IF HE HAD LIVED
HE WOULD HAVE BURIED US ALL.
MR. COOPER WAS A SNOOPER.

"My heavens," said Madame Marie. "Rather disrespectful, don't you think?"

"Yes, ma'am. But in 1873 I suppose the wounds of the Civil War had not yet fully healed. Mr. Cooper had, as you see, fought for the CSA."

"The CSA?"

"The Confederate States of America. He made the unfortunate mistake of dying too far north."

37

Madame Marie closed her eyes and clutched the edges of the miniature headstone.

"Speak through me, Mr. Cooper. Speak through me!"

She had already laid out her séance tools: candles, sketch pad, sharpened pencils, and her "spirit slates," two chalkboards bound together that, when opened, would reveal messages written by those on the far side of the grave.

"I am here to be your voice," said Madame Marie, releasing her grip on the stone and sinking deeper into her trance. Gazing off at some unseen middle distance, she sat cross-legged on the grass, placed the sketch pad in her lap.

Eddie handed her a pencil.

She gripped it in her fist without even looking at it and let it hover in circles over the first sheet of paper. "Let your words flow through me, Mr. Cooper! Speak through me now!"

Her pencil touched the paper. Seemingly powered by an unseen force, it scratched out rings of overlapping circles.

And then Madame Marie's hand automatically wrote a single word:

CHILD

"Find a child," she said in a faint, wispy voice that wasn't her own.

The pencil spun out more circles.

"Young enough to communicate with spirits."

The pencil scraped across the pad.

YOUNG

"Like Seth Donnelly."

SETH

"A ghost seer."

SEER

"For I cannot speak to you directly. But through the child you will find the gold."

GOLD

The pencil point snapped.

Madame Marie's eyes flew open. She gasped.

"Oh, my. What happened?"

"Nothing, ma'am. Although I believe you may have overexerted yourself. You passed out."

"I am so sorry." Eddie held out his hand and helped Madame Marie stand. "I felt certain I had made contact. I felt the tingling. . . ."

She glanced down at the sketch pad and saw the words she boldly scribbled.

"Gold?" she said. "Oh, my."

Eddie didn't need to call his boss.

He knew it was time for Madame Marie to have an accident.

38

The next morning, at school, when Zack opened his locker, Mr. Willoughby was already inside it waiting for him.

"Ah, good morning, Zachary. I trust you slept well last night?"

Not really.

Zack had fallen asleep worrying about how he was going to tell the gym teacher about Chuck Buckingham's heart condition without sounding like a wacko.

"I heard a bit of troubling news this morning on the zombie front."

Zack closed the locker door on himself as tight as he could without chopping off his own head. "Such as?"

"Apparently," said Mr. Willoughby, "there's a new one."

"What?"

"A new zombie."

"There's two?"

"Precisely."

"How?"

"We can't say for certain. Suffice it to say, a young man wandered where he should not have . . ."

"And got bit by zombie number one."

"Yes! How did you know that?"

"Davy told me: If you're bitten by a zombie but somehow escape, you turn into a zombie, too. So what do we do?"

"No immediate action need be taken, but extra precautions will be put into place. You will undoubtedly notice increased guardianship activity."

"More ghosts?"

Mr. Willoughby nodded grimly.

"Okay. I gotta head to homeroom. Thanks for watching out for me."

Mr. Willoughby looked pleased when Zack said that. "Thank *you*, Zachary. Much to my surprise, doing good actually *feels* good!"

Zack grabbed his books.

Directly across the hall, a panicked fifth-grade girl was frantically opening and closing her locker.

"Where is it?" she muttered as she tore through her stuff. Out came books, a jacket, a bulky purple backpack. "I am so dead! If I don't find it . . . I . . . am . . . dead!"

She was becoming hysterical—as in crazy, not funny.

"Poor girl," sighed a soft voice beside Zack. "She can't find her homework. Again."

Zack turned. Another ghost. One he'd never met before. A sweet little lady with a hamburger bun of white hair on top of her head. She was wearing a Kiss the Cook apron.

"Alyssa is my granddaughter. I'm her guardian."

Zack nodded. He was standing in the middle of a crowded corridor. If he started talking to the empty air, everybody in the place would think he either was mental or had a hands-free cell phone.

"Would you mind? The paper she's looking for is in the side flap of her backpack. On the right, there."

Zack walked across the hall and tapped the girl (who was now tugging at her hair with both hands and dangerously close to yanking it all out) on the shoulder.

"Hey, did you check the side flap of your backpack? The one on the right, there?"

First the girl stared at Zack like he was crazy.

Then she practically ripped the zipper out of its seams. She found a single sheet of paper and nearly burst into tears of joy.

"Yes! I am so not dead! Thank you!"

"No problem."

Zack headed up the hall.

"How'd you know where to find it?" the girl called after him.

"Lucky guess," Zack said with a shrug. He turned to give Alyssa's grandmother a wink but the ghost was already gone.

39

On the way to homeroom, Zack saw Ms. DuBois and asked her what she'd do if she thought somebody might be too sick to take gym.

"Well, Zack, I believe I would air my suspicions to Ms. Rodgers, the school nurse."

So between homeroom and math, Zack did.

"I think there might be something wrong with his heart."

"And what makes you say that?" asked the nurse, who seemed genuinely concerned.

"I saw him running," said Zack, spinning a quick fib. "He got winded really, really fast. Like in two seconds and he's not overweight or anything, either."

"I see," said Ms. Rodgers, reaching for the stethoscope hanging on the coatrack. "Thank you, Mr. Jennings. I'll look into it."

"Maybe Chuck shouldn't go to gym class today. . . ."

"I'll look into it, Mr. Jennings."

• • •

130

At lunchtime, Zack's table in the cafeteria grew a little more crowded.

Ms. DuBois was there, eating carrots and hummus. So were Azalea, Malik, Benny, and Chuck. They were joined by newcomer Alyssa, who just had to eat lunch with Zack. "Because he so totally saved my life this morning!" she said.

"Wow, Zack," said Malik, "perhaps we are becoming the cool kids!"

Azalea scoffed at that. "Dream on."

"Have you met any new friends, Azalea?" asked Ms. DuBois.

"Why bother? My dad's in the army. We'll be moving at the end of the school year. Maybe sooner. We move all the time."

"Uh-oh," said Chuck, slumping down in his seat, apparently trying to disappear.

Two teachers approached the table. Zack recognized Ms. Rodgers, the nurse. She was walking with a guy wearing blue gym shorts and a gray Pettimore Yankees T-shirt. There was a whistle around his neck; Ms. Rodgers had the stethoscope around hers.

Gym Shorts stuck his hands on his hips. Melon-sized muscles bulged on his arms, his legs, even his neck.

"Which one is he?" he asked.

"That's Charles Buckingham," said the nurse. "Hello again, Chuck."

"Uh, hi, Ms. Rodgers," he said shyly.

"Your mother is calling your family physician," Ms. Rodgers said in her most soothing nurse voice. "Everything's going to be fine but we might want to send you home a little early today."

"Okay."

"And no gym class. Not for a while."

Chuck smiled nervously. "Okay."

"Where's the other one?" barked the man in the gym shorts. His thighs were as wide as stuffed turkeys.

The nurse pointed at Zack.

"Zack Jennings?"

"Yes, sir."

"I'm Coach Mike. Phys ed." He checked his clipboard. "Looks like I've got you later this afternoon."

Zack gulped. "Yes, sir. Seventh period."

"Good. You need to put a little meat on those bones, son."

"Yes, sir."

"Is everything all right, Coach Mike?" asked Ms. DuBois.

"Everything's fine now, thanks to young Mr. Jennings. The boy has a sixth sense like those dogs that can sniff out diseases. You catch that on the news last night?"

"Sorry, no," said Ms. DuBois. "But whatever did Zack do?"

"I'll tell you what he did." Coach Mike hiked up his gym shorts for emphasis. "He alerted us to his buddy's irregular heartbeat."

"It may just be a murmur," added the nurse. "But it might suggest something more serious. Either way, we should play it safe until we know for sure."

"So you see, Zack?" said Coach Mike. "You might've saved your pal's life today."

"He saved mine, too!" said Alyssa. "First thing this morning!"

The gym teacher thrust out his hand. "I just wanted to say well done, Mr. Jennings. Keep up the good work. See you in seventh period. We're gonna make you some muscles!"

"Thanks," said Zack. Mr. Willoughby was definitely right: It felt good to do good.

And then, over the spiky top of the gym teacher's buzz cut, Zack saw the ghost of Bartholomew Buckingham dip into a long, gracious bow.

He had dropped by to say thanks, too.

That made Zack feel even better.

The next three weeks flew by.

Almost every day, Zack bumped into a new guardian ghost sent to protect a family member from the potential zombie threat. Some of the ghosts Zack knew, like Kathleen Williams, who he'd met over the summer at the crossroads and again at the Hanging Hill Playhouse. She had been a nightclub and Broadway musical star back in the 1950s. Turned out her great-great-grandniece, Laurel Jumper, was a sixth grader at Pettimore Middle School.

"I heard her singing in the shower this morning," the ghost gushed. "She has a *marvelous* voice. Simply marvelous! I only wish she believed in her talent enough to try out for the school choral group! Laurel could be a star on Broadway! A star!"

So Zack found Laurel and made a few subtle suggestions. Laurel auditioned for the school chorus and was, of course, snapped up right away. She even had a solo in the upcoming fall concert.

Laurel Jumper and other kids Zack helped joined his lunch bunch in the cafeteria, which had grown so large he and Malik had had to drag two tables together to make sure everybody had a seat.

Judy volunteered as a class mom a couple of times and got to meet a few of the ghosts. Bartholomew Buckingham gave her tips on how to make *Curiosity Cat* more Shakespearean.

"I saw your show," he told her. "Jolly good fun. But perhaps you might consider having a few of your cats duel each other in the final act?" He then put on a brief demonstration of feline fight choreography. There was a lot of leaping, prancing, hissing, and posing.

Judy told him she'd think about it.

Benny had new ideas every day (except when Judy was the class mom) about what Zack should blow up next.

Azalea depressed everybody with gloomy poems she wrote (but she always winked to let Zack and Malik know she was messing with their heads).

Chuck Buckingham's irregular heartbeat turned out to be a pretty common heart murmur, so he could take gym class, which he and Zack were actually enjoying, because Coach Mike—despite the whistle, shorts, and buzz cut—wasn't the typical P.E. teacher. More encouraging, less screaming. By the fourth week of September, when Zack flexed his arm, he could swear he saw a muscle bump.

Assistant Principal Crumpler was grouchier than usual, because Wade Muggins, the school's custodian, had "gone AWOL"—which Zack found out from Azalea was an army term for not showing up to do your job. There was a new janitor every week. They all kept quitting. None of them could stand working for Mr. Crumpler.

Ms. DuBois ate at Zack's table whenever she was on cafeteria duty. So did Ms. Rodgers, the school nurse.

Even Kyle Snertz, Kurt's younger brother, was sitting at the table and he wasn't mumbling anymore, either. In fact, he was pretty funny. Everybody swore he would be a stand-up comic on TV someday and he said, "Wow, maybe I will."

And so far, his big brother, Kurt Snertz—who said he hated Zack even more for turning his little brother into a "nerd loser"—hadn't made good on his multiple threats to stick Zack's head down a toilet.

Some days, after school, almost half of the sixth grade would hang out at Zack's house. (Well, it felt like almost half.) Everybody wanted to meet Zack's famous stepmom, Judy Magruder, because they had all grown up reading her *Curiosity Cat* books. They all liked Zipper, too.

Yep, for the first time in his life, Zack Jennings was cool.

He was also popular—well, at least with all the other *unpopular* kids, who, come to think of it, always outnumbered the popular kids anyhow. There could be only one star quarterback, one head cheerleader. There were tons of geeks, nerds, dorks, and dweebs. That was probably why they had so many names for being different.

All in all, September was a totally awesome month.

Then, in early October, Zipper got lonely.

Zipper stood on the couch, gazing out the window.

Watching Zack disappear. Again.

His tail wilted.

Where did his boy go every morning, five days in a row?

Was it more fun than staying home and throwing the squishy ball in the backyard?

More exciting than pretending they were on a safari?

More laughs than when all the other boys and girls came by the house and Zipper showed them his tricks?

Hey, where were all those other kids during the day?

Did they go to the same place Zack went?

If so, it must be a fun place.

Very fun.

More fun than the house without Zack.

Zipper sniffed.

Zack's scent was easy to pick up, even though Judy was burning toast in the kitchen again and the neighbors had just mowed their lawn, because Zack was his extra-special person. Every dog has one. Zack was his.

Zipper tiptoed through the kitchen.

"Going out, Zip?" Judy said as his nails clacked crisply on the tile floor.

Zipper gave her a quick yap and a tail wag.

"Have fun," she said. "Just don't water my rosebushes for me."

He gave her another yap, this one signaling he understood where the approved rest areas were located in the backyard. He stepped through the flapping doggy door.

Judy and George had taught him not to stray beyond the backyard when he went out to do his business. Not to bother the neighbors or venture into the street.

But that had been before Zack started disappearing every morning.

Zipper sniffed twice.

Zack's scent was in the wind.

All Zipper had to do was follow it.

So he did.

Eddie strode into the main entrance of the school and found Assistant Principal Crumpler's office, just like the boss had told him to.

It was upstairs in the building that had once been Horace P. Pettimore's mansion.

He rapped his knuckles on the bald man's half-open door.

"What?"

"I'm your new janitor, sir."

"Humph. How long do you plan to stay on the job? A day?"

"As long as you need me, sir."

"Humph." Mr. Crumpler stood up from his desk and clipped a walkie-talkie to his belt, muttering the whole time: "Lousy board of education. Think I should unclog my own toilets . . . cafeteria tray washer flooding . . . lima beans on the floor . . . sloppy joes . . ."

That was enough to get them out the door and headed down the sweeping staircase to the main hall.

"Do I have an office?" Eddie asked.

"You don't need an office! You need a mop! A bucket!"

"Yes, sir."

Eddie was wearing a green shirt over green work pants and had a ring of keys clipped to his belt. He looked very janitorial. The boss wanted him at the school because that was where they had the best chance of finding the special child the spirit of John Lee Cooper had spoken of through the medium.

Eddie and Crumpler reached the grand foyer.

"Mighty fine oil painting," said Eddie, admiring the large portrait of Horace Pettimore in its gilded frame.

The bald man propped his hands on his hips and sized Eddie up.

"You're not from around here, are you?"

"No, sir."

"That why you talk like you have molasses in your mouth?"

"I suppose so. I hail from Chattanooga, Tennessee, which, coincidentally, is very close to the Georgia border."

"So?"

"Just makin' small talk."

"Well, knock it off! You've got work to do!"

"Yes, sir, Mr. Crumpler."

Eddie wouldn't say another word.

He wouldn't point out that he came from a city extremely close to the Georgia home of Patrick J. Cooper, the hero teacher who had died in this very school, valiantly attempting to "save" the two Donnelly brothers in the smoky corridor.

Another terrible "accident."

He chuckled quietly.

And that was when the small dog darted through the front doors Eddie must have forgotten to close when he'd entered the building.

"Mrs. Pochinko?" Mr. Crumpler yelled into his walkie-talkie. "Alert animal control! We need a tranquilizer gun!"

He and the new janitor had chased the dog west, out of the main hall, past a few classrooms, up the steps, and into the cafeteria.

The fifth graders, who ate earliest, were squealing with delight as the mangy mutt scampered under their tables.

"Stop! Bad dog! Bad dog!" Mr. Crumpler was screaming. The bewildered children stared at him. "Eat your vegetables!" he hollered. "Eat them now!" He punched the talk button on his radio again. "Mrs. Pochinko?"

"*Sir?*"

"Give me a hallway lockdown. Give it to me now!"

"*On it, sir.*"

Mr. Crumpler stood frozen, mopping the top of his bald head with a paper napkin he had swiped from a boy who looked like he used his shirt sleeve instead of his napkin anyway.

This was Carl D. Crumpler's worst nightmare come

true. A wild dog running amuck, jeopardizing the safety of all his students. Chaos. Rabies. Armageddon.

"You think maybe we should chase after it?" asked the rookie janitor.

Crumpler gave the man a look. "You bet I do, mush mouth!"

When Zipper sprang through the open door and leapt up onto Zack's desk, the whole classroom cracked up.

When the dog started licking his face like he was a ham-flavored ice cream cone, they went wild.

"Friend of yours?" asked Ms. DuBois.

"Yes, ma'am. This is Zipper. I guess he missed me."

That was all he got to say before Mrs. Pochinko started braying over the PA: *"Teachers, students, please stay in your classrooms. There is an animal control issue in the hallways. Mr. Crumpler has the situation under . . . eh . . . he's working on it. . . ."*

"Uh-oh," said Ms. DuBois.

Malik raised his hand.

"Yes, Mr. Sherman?"

"If animal control comes, they will undoubtedly want to take Zipper to the dog pound. I think it would be wise for us to hide him."

"Where?" asked Ms. DuBois.

"We'll find a place," said Zack.

Ms. DuBois gestured for them to hurry. "Go on, boys.

I'll call your mother, Zack, to tell her to swing by and pick up the dog. Meet her out front in the visitor parking lot after the next bell."

"Thanks, Ms. DuBois! You're the best!"

"Hurry! Before Mr. Crumpler sees you!"

So Zack grabbed Zipper; then he and Malik hightailed it out the door.

Mr. Crumpler and his new janitor, Captain Cornpone, had cleared the cafeteria and the wood shop and had entered the infamous smoky corridor when he noticed an open door.

The DuBois woman's classroom.

"This way!" he said, and they stepped inside.

"Hello, Mr. Crumpler," said the history teacher, who had the same sort of Southern drawl as the new mop pusher.

"Your door. Has it been open long?"

"Not very."

The classroom was full of students. Two desks, however, were suspiciously empty.

"Is there some sort of problem?" asked Ms. DuBois.

"Yes!" said Mr. Crumpler. "I am looking for a dog. Have you seen one?"

Ms. DuBois rubbed her chin thoughtfully. "A dog? Hmmm . . ."

Some of the kids giggled.

"Oh, you mean that sweet little pooch who just jumped out our window?"

"What?"

"Heavens, I almost forgot. See, we had the window open—this old room gets stuffy sometimes—and all of a sudden, out of nowhere, the cutest little doggy you ever did see comes scootin' through that door, zips up the center aisle, and with a hop, skip, and a jump leaps out the back window."

"You let him get away?"

"Why, we barely knew he was here before, zip, he was gone."

"Which way did it go?"

"Heavens, I couldn't say."

Mr. Crumpler narrowed his eyes. "Who sits in those two seats?"

"The two empty desks?"

"That's right."

"Nobody. I believe that is why they are empty."

The children looked ready to giggle again.

So Mr. Crumpler gave them his glare. The one that said, *I'll see you all in detention hall if you so much as breathe!*

That shut 'em up.

"If the dog returns, call the office!"

"Yes, sir."

Mr. Crumpler straightened his tie and strode out the door.

When he hit the hall, he wasn't sure, but he thought he might've heard children tittering behind him.

No. That was impossible.

The children feared Carl D. Crumpler far too much to laugh at him behind his back.

"We should head downstairs and double back!" shouted Zack, hugging Zipper close to his chest.

The dog kept licking him. First the chin. Then the nose.

"Excellent idea!" said Malik.

They raced down a staircase to the basement.

"We need to stay close to the main entrance!"

"Well, we can't take him up to the cafeteria," said Malik. "And if we head out to the parking lot too early, Mr. Crumpler might see us."

"How about the janitor's closet?" said Zack.

"Excellent! It's dead ahead. Is it unlocked?"

Zack jiggled the knob. "Yes!"

"Hurry."

They scurried into the dark room and closed the door.

"Lights?" Malik asked.

"No," said Zack. "Someone might see it under the door."

Zipper grumbled and squirmed, so Zack put him down on the ground.

"Stay right here, Zip, okay? Judy's on her way. How much time till the bell?"

Malik pushed a button on his wristwatch and the numbers glowed. "Twenty-five minutes."

Zack exhaled. "Ms. DuBois is so cool . . . covering for us."

"Yeah."

And then the boys heard the *tick-tick-tick* of dog claws on concrete.

"Zipper?" Zack said in a tense whisper. "Come back here. Zip? Zipper!"

Zipper started to whine. And then scratch. And then dig the way he did when his ball got stuck in the corner of the couch.

A flashlight clicked on.

"I found it on a shelf," said Malik. He handed it to Zack.

Zack shone the beam over to where Zipper was pawing furiously at the leg of an industrial shelving unit crammed with jugs and bottles and boxes of toilet paper.

"Zipper? You've got to be quiet. There's no food on those shelves. It isn't like the pantry. It's just a bunch of janitor junk."

Zack leaned on the shelving unit to make his point.

"Leave it alone."

And when he let go, the whole steel rack slid forward.

"Wow! What is that?" asked Malik, who had grabbed a second flashlight and was examining the opening in the wall.

"I dunno," said Zack. "Some kind of secret entrance?"

"To what?"

"Good question. Come on! But watch your step. There's a low stone wall." He stepped over the short barrier and sniffed the air. "It smells different back here."

"Indeed," said Malik. "Earthy."

Wooden, not steel, shelves lined the walls on the other side of the secret entryway. A few held old-fashioned glass jars. Malik picked one up. Blew the dust off the lid. "'Wild indigo root compound,'" he read. "'Prepared 1875.' Amazing. This must be the root cellar for the old Pettimore estate. This is where they would store food for the winter."

"Zipper must've liked the smells leaking under the hidden panel." Zack swung the flashlight across the dirt floor. "Zip? Zip?"

Finally, the light hit Zipper. He was standing in front of a hole in the stone wall, pawing at something on the ground.

"What'd you find this time? An antique cheeseburger?"

Zipper whimpered and kept scratching at the ground.

"What is it, boy?" Zack asked.

And then he and Malik saw what Zipper had just uncovered.

"Well," said Zack, "the middle part is obviously a warning, like a No Trespassing sign. But the rest? Maybe they're Egyptian hieroglyphics or something."

"No," gasped Malik. "It's code!"

They studied what someone had carved into the stone:

⌐ ∧⊓⌐⌐⌐⌐⌐⌐ ⌐⌐⌐⌐⌐ ⌐∧ ⌐⌐⌐⌐⌐⌐ <⌐⌐⌐

TURN BACK NOW OR DESCEND INTO HELL

⌐⌐<∧ ∨∨⌐⌐ <⌐∨⌐⌐ ⌐⌐⌐⌐ ⌐ ∨⌐⌐⌐⌐ ∨⌐⌐>⌐⌐

⌐⌐⌐ ∧⊓>⌐ ⌐⌐⌐∨∧⌐⌐∨∨ ∨⌐⌐⌐⌐ ⌐⌐ >⌐⌐∧ ⌐⊓⊓⌐

"It appears to be a diagrammatic cipher," said Malik. "Huh?"

"It substitutes symbols for letters instead of letters for letters as you might find on a decoder ring."

"What's it say?"

"Not certain. But I believe the coder is using what is called the pigpen cipher, a substitution code often used by the Masons. Each clustering of letters indicates a new word. . . ."

"How much time do we have until the bell rings?"

Malik checked his watch. "Not much. Perhaps I should take a rubbing of the inscription. That way, we can finish cracking the code at a more convenient time."

"Yeah," said Zack.

"We need a sheet of paper and a crayon of some kind."

Zack scanned the room with his flashlight. On the wall he saw some rock concert posters and another one of those prints of Horace Pettimore. They might work. Then, on a rack, he saw a stack of brown paper grocery sacks. "There's your paper!"

"Excellent!" Malik grabbed a bag and tore out a flat panel.

Zack turned his flashlight left. Saw more jars of pickled preserves. A pile of moldy potatoes. A stack of candles, some white, some black.

"Hey, how about a black candle for your crayon?"

"Perfect! I should be able to pick up the impressions using the same technique one would employ to do a gravestone rubbing."

"Do you need the light?"

"No."

Malik started rubbing. Zack moved his flashlight beam up to the jagged hole in the wall just past the spot where they'd found the secret message. The fieldstones circling the three-foot-wide opening were scorched black. Zipper sniffed the edges.

"Careful, boy," said Zack. He didn't want Zipper falling

through the hole. There was some kind of chute, like an enclosed playground slide, on the other side. Maybe that was what the warning was all about: descending into whatever hell was down there in the darkness.

He couldn't risk it. Zack scooped his dog off the ground. Cradled him in his arms.

"Finished!" said Malik.

"Great. How much time till the bell?"

Malik rolled up his paper and checked his watch. "Two minutes."

"Okay, Zipper, under my shirt. We need to smuggle you out of the building."

The boys made their way through the swiveling shelves to the janitor's closet—shoving the shelf unit back into place.

And then, at the sound of the bell, they ran out the door faster than either one of them had ever run before.

Horace Pettimore had not been this joyful in ages.

Not since the steamy Louisiana night when he'd stolen sixty-six dead men's souls and sealed them up inside glass jars.

He had just slipped into the portrait hanging on the wall of the old root cellar, where he observed the new boy, the one with a long family history in this corner of Connecticut, as the boy discovered the secret marker.

It had to be a sign. An omen.

Zack had to be the one.

The one he had been seeking for more than a century. The one he had lured there with the buried voodoo charm.

The time was drawing nigh. Soon he would slip his soul into the boy's body and use it to retrieve his treasure.

Of course the scrawny child would lose his soul in the exchange, exactly twenty-four hours after Pettimore's soul shoved it out of the boy's body.

But that did not matter.

Because Captain Horace P. Pettimore would live again!

"Hi, Mom! You remember Ms. DuBois?"

"Sure."

Zack didn't have time for much more than a quick pass off of Zipper through an open car window.

"I am so sorry about this," Judy said to Ms. DuBois.

"I'm sure Zipper just missed Zack," said Ms. DuBois. "No harm, no foul, as they say."

"From now on, he doesn't go outside without body-guards."

"Well, we best hurry back inside," said Ms. DuBois. "If we're not in the cafeteria for our lunch period, Mr. Crumpler might become suspicious."

"Thanks, Mom," Zack said.

Judy blew him a quick kiss. Zipper had his paws pressed against the edge of the window, a huge smile on his snout.

"You're riding shotgun, pal." Judy picked Zip up and placed him on the passenger seat. "In fact, you might want to lie low until we clear the school zone."

Zipper seemed to understand. He hopped down to the

floorboard, where he hunkered on the rubber mat, head tucked between paws in sneak-attack mode.

"See you after school, Zack!" Judy said as she pulled away.

"See you, Mom!"

"Love you!"

"Love you, too!"

The second bell rang.

"Come on, Zack," said Ms. DuBois. "Back inside. So, where did you boys hide?"

Zack was just about to tell Ms. DuBois about the swiveling supply shelf in the janitor's closet and the root cellar and the cool carved stone when he saw Mr. Willoughby walk through a door. Not a doorway, a door.

He was shaking his head and mouthing a single word over and over: "No!"

"Um, here and there. No place special."

"Well," said Ms. DuBois, "it worked!"

Yeah.

But apparently, Zack couldn't tell any grown-ups about the root cellar, either!

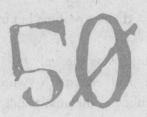

Zack's terrible day got even worse after school officially ended.

His final class was technology education with another really cool teacher, named Mr. Bill Green, who told them that starting the next day, they'd each be designing, engineering, and constructing a ping-pong catapult to do a trajectory-analysis project.

"That should be fun!" said Malik as he and Zack headed up the crowded corridor toward their lockers. Everywhere Zack looked, he (and no one else) saw guardian ghosts. Some were escorting their relatives up and down the hall. Others were hanging out inside open lockers. One was trying to get a drink from a water fountain but her palm kept passing through the on button.

Two, who looked like a mismatched set—one a lady in a bright green dress, the other a man in a funny bowler hat, both with bullet holes in the center of their heads— stood behind the newest janitor, who was working a push broom down the hall. The newly arrived ghosts were holding their noses and shouting stuff like "Stay away from this one!" and "He's nothing but trouble!" to anyone who'd listen.

Zack, of course, was the only one who could listen, and frankly, he had enough to worry about without adding a new janitor to the mix, thank you very much.

The couple followed the janitor, blowing unheard raspberries at him as he swept the corridor clean.

Zack and Malik were headed the other way.

They pulled open a door and there was Azalea Torres, working her locker open on the wall outside Ms. DuBois's classroom.

"Hey, you guys! I just had this awesome idea. It's October already. Halloween's coming. We should go on a cemetery crawl!"

"What's that?" asked Zack.

"Well, you go to a graveyard and take rubbings off the headstones. Some of the inscriptions are wicked funny, like 'Here lies the body of Jonathan Blake, Stepped on the gas instead of the brake.'"

"That would make an awesome field trip for our history class!" said Malik.

"Yeah," said Azalea. "I already talked to Ms. DuBois and she said it was an awesome idea, too! We just need to pick a date."

"The sooner, the better," said Malik. "The rubbings would make excellent Halloween decorations."

"Yeah," said Zack. "We could hang them on our lockers, which kind of resemble caskets."

Malik's and Azalea's smiles instantly curdled into frowns.

"What? Okay. You don't like the locker-coffin idea. We could—"

Someone grabbed his belt from behind and hoisted him off the ground.

"Well, if it isn't wacky little Zacky."

Kurt Snertz.

So that was why his friends had stopped smiling so fast.

"You ready for your toilet swirly, wimp?"

51

Kurt Snertz must've spent all month plotting his revenge.

When Kurt let go of his belt and Zack spun around, he could see that Snertz had *four* guys with him this time. Zack had Azalea and Malik.

"Leave him alone!" shouted Azalea.

"What? You got girls fighting your fights for you these days, Jennings? You are such a wimpy wuss! Good thing we're so close to the girls' bathroom—the one you probably use all the time. Six toilets, no waiting. One swishy coming right up!"

His thug friends snickered.

"Stop this," said Malik. "I'll call the police!"

"Shut up, Lick-Me. Or you're next!"

"I told you before," said Zack. "Leave Malik out of this! Azalea, too! If you're still mad about what I did to your little brother last summer . . . ."

"Nah. I'm mad about what you've done to him this month! A Snertz eating at the nerd table? Cracking jokes and back-talking to *me*? You ruined him, Jennings! So now I'm gonna ruin you!"

Snertz cracked his knuckles.

Flexed his fingers.

Balled his hand into a fist.

"So, wussy boy, you know any prayers?"

Another movie unspooled in Zack's brain: with Errol Flynn as Robin Hood. "Yes, and I'll say one for you!"

Some of Snertz's bully buddies actually laughed at the snap.

But not Snertz.

Veins bulged on his arm and in his neck.

"I hope you enjoyed that, Jennings. Because those are the last words you are ever gonna say!"

Snertz cocked back his fist.

That was when Malik stomped down as hard as he could on Snertz's shoe and Azalea grabbed Zack by the arm.

Snertz wailed in agony.

"Run for it!" shouted Malik. "Hurry!"

"In here," shouted Azalea. "Quick!"

"What?"

She shoved him through a swinging door.

The girls' bathroom!

"Wait!" said Zack. "We're trapped."

"MR. SNERTZ?" boomed a loud voice out in the hall.

Zack stuck his ear to the bathroom door and could hear Snertz's buddies running away.

The big voice boomed again. "WHY WERE YOU ABOUT TO GO INTO THE GIRLS' BATHROOM?" Mr. Green. The tech ed teacher. He had the loudest voice and biggest muscles of all the teachers in the school.

"I lost somethin'."

"IN THE *GIRLS'* ROOM?"

"Um . . ."

"YOU'RE SUPPOSED TO BE IN ROOM NINETY-THREE. DETENTION HALL! WITH ME! MOVE IT."

"I'll be back!" Snertz shouted.

"BACK FOR WHAT?"

"Nothin'."

"YOU DO KNOW I COACH WRESTLING *AND* BOXING, RIGHT?"

"Yes, sir."

Zack heard Snertz and Mr. Green walking away.

Five seconds later, there was a knock on the door.

"Hey, you guys? It's me!"

Malik.

Azalea pulled open the door, grabbed Malik's arm, and yanked him into the bathroom. Fortunately, the bathroom had been empty when Zack and Azalea had first burst through the doors.

"We should probably hide in here a little longer," Azalea suggested. "Just in case Snertz overpowers Mr. Green and pulls a jailbreak."

Zack and Malik nodded slowly. Azalea had a way of making things way overdramatic.

"So, either of you guys ever been in the girls' room before?" Azalea asked in a hushed tone.

Both shook their heads.

"I've been inside the boys' room lots of times," she said. "It's nothing special." She moved to the row of sinks and mirrors. "It's not haunted like this one is."

"This bathroom is haunted?" asked Malik.

Azalea nodded ominously. "Bloody Mary. You ever heard of her?"

"Um, I don't think so. . . ."

"Who is she?" asked Zack.

"No one knows for sure. Some say she's a little girl who was buried alive. Others say it's the ghost of crazy Mary O'Malley!"

"Who?" asked Zack.

"This crazy Irish cleaning lady who used to scrub floors with babies!"

Zack nodded. "Oh. Her."

"But most agree—Bloody Mary is Mary Tudor, the saddest queen of England ever, a lady who had five babies die on her and doesn't like it if you make fun of her and her dead kids."

"Question," said Malik.

"What?"

"Why would the ghost of the former queen of England choose to haunt the girls' bathroom in a middle school in Connecticut in America?"

"Turn off the lights! You'll see."

Azalea pulled a black candle out of her backpack. Lit it.

Zack shrugged. What the heck? They had to kill a little time to make sure the hallway was totally clear. He flicked the switch.

"Come on, you guys," said Azalea. "Move closer to the sinks. Stare into the mirror!"

Zack and Malik followed Azalea and stared at their own flickering reflections in the bathroom mirror.

"Now, all we have to do is say, 'Bloody Mary, I have your children,' five times real fast while turning around in circles!"

"And then what happens?" asked Malik.

"Bloody Mary comes screaming out of the mirror and scratches our eyeballs out of our heads!"

"And this is fun exactly how?"

"It just is!"

"Come on, Malik," said Zack. "Azalea needs our help."

He was thinking that the sooner the three of them spun

around in a circle five times, the sooner they could all go home.

Malik nodded. "Very well, Azalea. Proceed."

"Okay. Say the words with me. Ready?"

"Ready."

"One, two, three . . ."

"Bloody Mary, I have your children!"

They turned around in a circle.

"Bloody Mary, I have your children!"

They made another circle in front of the mirror.

"Bloody Mary . . ."

Zack stopped.

Because someone appeared in the mirror.

And it wasn't the queen of England.

Zack stared blankly at the mirror.

Azalea and Malik were speaking to him but their voices sounded like they were underwater.

Zack's eyes were riveted on the mysterious figure wavering inside the mirror, a young woman wearing a wreath of white leaves in her raven black hair, long white gloves, and a ruffled white wedding gown that made her look like a bell.

"I am Azalea's guardian," the ghost said in a woeful whisper. "She is in grave danger."

"Is it the zombie?" said Zack.

He felt Azalea nudge him in the ribs when he said that.

"No, but I cannot say his name, for were he to hear it spoken, all would be lost."

Zack nodded. He understood. Sort of.

"Guard Azalea. Do not let her fall into the evil demon's clutches, for if she does, within the day, she will surely lose her soul."

"Who are you? What's your name?"

Azalea nudged him in the ribs again and said something

like "You're just pretending" and laughed, so Zack laughed, too, even though the woman in the mirror was weeping.

"I am but an outcast daughter. A weeping widow. A great-great-great-great-great-great-great-great-grandmother."

All those greats made Zack gulp.

"My name is Mary. Mary Jane Hopkins."

At the very same moment, in the French Quarter of New Orleans, an eight-year-old girl with caramel-colored skin and a bright yellow kerchief wrapped around her head strolled into her aunt's kitchen.

The older woman was sipping chicory-flavored coffee from a demitasse cup and had been enjoying a freshly fried and lightly powdered beignet. She put them both aside when she saw the look in the little girl's eyes.

"What is it, child?" the aunt asked in a whisper.

The little girl smiled. "The time has come, Auntie. We must travel north. Tonight. Now."

"Connecticut?"

The child's smile grew even broader. "Connecticut."

"Sorry, I was just goofing around," Zack said for the tenth time.

He, Azalea, and Malik were on the bus, headed home.

"Why did you ask if Bloody Mary was a zombie?" asked Azalea, laughing so hard she had to hold on to her sides. "Was that like even one of the options?"

"I dunno," said Zack.

"And then," said Malik, short of breath from giggling, "you kept saying 'What is your name?' when, obviously, it was supposed to be Mary!"

Zack went ahead and laughed along with his two friends, who were more or less laughing at him. Hey, it beat explaining what he'd really seen.

Azalea wiped some of the laugh tears out of her eyes, smudging her makeup as she did. "You guys hanging out at Zack's today?"

"Nah," said Zack. "We need to do some junk at Malik's house."

"Okay. Cool. Have you done your family tree, yet?"

"Oh, yes," said Malik. "My father and mother helped me last weekend."

"Yeah," said Zack, "mine, too."

The bus came to a stop. "What's the matter with you guys? Haven't you ever heard about waiting till the last possible minute to do anything?"

Zack laughed. "You're doing yours tonight, right?"

"Yep. Because they're not due until *tomorrow*. See ya!"

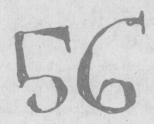

The Donnelly brothers had been working with Seth's new zombie for more than a month.

"How come he only obeys you?" groused Joseph.

"Because I was the first human soul he came across after he got zombie-bit, I guess."

Joseph balled up his fist like he was going to give his little brother a good walloping. "You'll make him do whatever I tell you to make him do, right?"

"Sure, I will. You're all the family I got, Joe."

"And don't you forget it, boy-o! We're never gonna let some grown-up get the better of us again, are we?"

"No, Joe. We're gonna get the better of them!"

Joe swung out his arm, but instead of punching his brother, he draped it over Seth's shoulder. "You and me. We're all we got. Together, we're gonna make some dumb grown-up pay for what that Mr. Cooper done to us."

"Then can we move on, Joe?"

"Maybe."

"I'd like to meet my mom and dad."

"I said maybe! First we need us our revenge!"

"Okay. How do we kill a grown-up so we can head home?"

Joseph gestured at the steam boiler. "See that thing? It used to be on Captain Pettimore's paddle wheeler."

"Sure, I remember. Mr. Cooper told us all about Pettimore."

"Why you think the captain put it down here so deep in his tunnels?"

Seth shrugged. "To heat the place?"

"Nah. He's dead. Don't need no heat. Use your noggin, dummy."

"Sorry."

"It's okay. You died too young. Didn't get to be as smart as me." Joseph walked over to the cold furnace. "See, we're real close to where the captain hid his gold."

"I know," said Seth, who didn't like it when his big brother said he was dumb. "I've seen it."

"Well, think about it. The chamber on the other side of that door there, the one the chimney pipe winds its way over to? That there has to be one of the captain's most ingenious defenses."

"How's it work?"

"Easy. His zombie chases a treasure hunter into this room; the man sees that chamber, runs in to hide. He slams the door shut, thinks he's safe. Meanwhile, the zombie lowers that lock bar, ambles on back to the boiler here, and sets in to stoking the furnace beneath the water tank. Zombie gets a real nice fire goin' with all that wood stacked up . . ."

"And all the smoke goes up the chimney and over to the locked chamber!"

"Bingo! The treasure hunter chokes, suffocates, and dies—just like we did." Joseph winked. "Your zombie gets to feast on smoked brains!"

Now Seth started training his zombie to do the things Joseph wanted done. Loading firewood into the fuel doors underneath the boiler tank. Greasing the hinges on the lock bar outside the smokehouse-chamber door.

"You do a good job," Seth told his zombie, "and I'll let you go upstairs for some real tasty treats."

"Yep," added Joseph, "all the kid brains you can eat! A whole school of 'em."

The zombie drooled.

"But you don't get nothin' but dried-up old carcasses and bones until we get us our revenge! Tell him, Seth!"

"You heard my brother?"

"Yes, master."

"Good," said Joseph. "Now, any Son of Daniel Boone will tell you, when setting a bear trap, the first thing you need to do is make sure it doesn't look like a trap to the bear!"

"Open that door for us," said Seth, indicating the heavy wooden door below the angled smokestack pipe.

The zombie opened the door and stepped into a small room, six feet wide, twelve feet long. The door on the far end was closed.

"That's it! You still got those fire sticks?"

The zombie pulled the box of matches out of his tattered trousers.

"Let's get this show on the road!" shouted Joseph.

The Donnelly brothers' simple trap was set.

Now all they needed was one grown-up dumb enough to stumble into it.

The way they'd been dumb enough to trust that murdering liar Mr. Cooper.

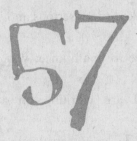

Zack and Malik got off the bus in a tidy cluster of modest homes.

"I should warn you, Zack," said Malik as they headed up the sidewalk. "My mother is currently confined to a wheelchair."

"Was she in an accident?"

"No. She has diabetic nephropathy. A progressive kidney disease."

"I'm sorry."

Malik forced his smile to widen. "She remains in good spirits. She is not a giver-upper. However, the doctors say she needs dialysis."

They climbed the steps to the front porch. Zack noticed a gap in the porch railings and a ramp made of pressure-treated lumber.

Malik swung open the door.

"Hi, Mom! Hi, Dad! This is my friend from school I told you about, Zack Jennings."

"Hello," said Zack timidly.

Malik's mom had a peaceful glow as she sat smiling in what appeared to be a secondhand wheelchair.

His father looked super-serious and sad, his hair speck-led with gray.

"Well, it's nice to finally meet you, Zack," said Mrs. Sherman.

"Zack and I are working on a project!" Malik announced.

"For school?" his mom asked enthusiastically.

"Yes, Mom."

"Well, isn't that wonderful?"

"Oh, this weekend," said Malik, "we're planning a history field trip to the Civil War cemetery!"

His father sighed. "What day?"

"Saturday."

"This going to become a regular thing, Son? School on the weekend?"

"I'm going, too," said Zack. "My folks can drive us."

"Can you stay for dinner tonight, Zack?"

"Maybe next week, Mom," said Malik. "I promised Zack that I'd have dinner at his house tonight. We were just going to grab a couple of my books first."

"This weekend activity going to help you get a scholar-ship, Son?" Malik's father asked, his eyes weary.

"I hope so, sir."

"Good! Because you're too smart to end up like me. You go to college. Become a doctor. Get a job they can't ever take away from you. You hear me, Malik?"

"Yes, sir."

Feeling nearly as sad as Mr. Sherman sounded, Zack followed Malik up the staircase and into Malik's bedroom.

When the door closed, Malik held back the tears he clearly didn't want Zack to see.

"My dad lost his job six months ago," he said bravely. "That's why he's home now. Why we can't afford the dialysis. Not yet, anyway."

"I'm sorry," said Zack.

"Don't worry. We're not giver-uppers. None of us."

fifteen minutes later, Zack, Malik, and Zipper were upstairs in Zack's bedroom.

Zipper hopped up to the computer desk by way of Zack's swivel chair so he could take the best angle to lick Malik's face.

"He does this every time I come over here!" Malik laughed as Zipper's tongue slurped across his face.

"Okay, Zip," said Zack as he sat in his chair and pulled over a second one for Malik. "Off!"

Zipper bounded to the ground, making sure he was close enough to Malik's legs for the visitor to scratch him behind his ears.

"Shall we get cracking?" said Malik.

"Sure."

Malik spread out the rubbing he had made off the stone.

"Yes," said Malik, studying the sharply angled figures in the cryptogram. "Definitely a pigpen cipher."

"How's it work?" asked Zack.

"First, you make a tic-tac-toe grid and an X."

Malik found a blank sheet of paper. Plucked a marker out of a cup. Drew the grid and the X.

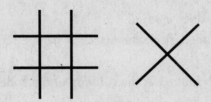

"Next," he said, "fill in each space with two letters."

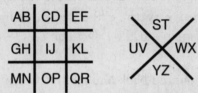

"The letters in each space are represented by the angled shape around them. The first is just the shape. For instance, an A would look like this." And he drew:

"The second letter gets the same shape but with an added dot. Therefore, B would be—"

See? Likewise, S and T would be—"

"Wow," marveled Zack. "It's simple."
"Sure. Once you know the secret."

"So what does it say?"

Malik handed Zack the marker. "You tell me!"

"Okay."

First Zack looked at the rubbing of the coded message.

⅃ ∧⊓⅃⊐ᄂ ⊐>⅃ᖷ⅄∨ ⅂∧ ∀ᖷ⅃⅃∨>ᖷ⅃ <ᄂᎬᎬ
TURN BACK NOW OR DESCEND INTO HELL
⅂ᄂ<∨ ∨∨⅃⅂⅄ <⅃∨∪⅃ ᖨᏫᄃᄂ ⅃ ∨⅃ᏫᏐⁿᖷ ∨⅃ⁿ>ᄂᎮ
⅃⅃⅄ ∧⊓>ᖷ Ꭾᖷⁿ∨ᖷᄂ∪∨∨ ∨⅃⅃ᎬᎬ ⅃ᄂ >ᄂᖷ∧ ⊐⊓⊓Ꭾ

His eyes bounced back and forth between the paper he was writing on and Malik's code key. He spelled out the first line:

A ZOMBIE GUARDS MY TREASURE WELL

Uh-oh, the zombie.

"Treasure!" said Malik. "Awesome."

Okay. Zack understood why Malik might be more interested in that part. Then again, he hadn't been the one talking with Davy and Mr. Willoughby.

"Of course," Malik continued, "whoever wrote it was most likely attempting to scare off any would-be treasure hunters. There are no such things as zombies in real life."

Zack just sort of nodded.

"It works quite nicely with the second line," Malik noted. "Interesting."

"What?"

"The 'turn back now' phrase suggests the stone we uncovered is situated close to the entry point for finding the treasure."

"The hole in the wall?"

"Precisely! Do the next bit, Zack."

"Okay."

Zack translated and then he and Malik read the entire inscription:

A ZOMBIE GUARDS MY TREASURE WELL
TURN BACK NOW OR DESCEND INTO HELL
NEXT STAND WATCH LIKE A SAILOR SHOULD
AND YOUR PROSPECTS SHALL BE VERY GOOD

"Well, that makes no sense," said Zack.

"Yes, it does," said Malik.

"What does it mean? 'Stand watch like a sailor should'?"

"It means one must look at the world as Captain Pettimore would have—if you want to find all his gold!"

Zack and Malik agreed to keep their discovery of the stone double-triple super secret—especially since the decoded warning had the word "treasure" in it.

"The thought of treasure and untold riches can drive people mad," said Malik, "make them do things they'd never think of doing."

"Yeah," said Zack. "Like eat bugs on TV."

Friday morning, Zack and Malik noticed that Azalea seemed extremely sad when she climbed aboard the school bus.

"Everything okay?" Zack asked.

She glared at him. "Not really. But then, we all can't have the perfectly happy little home like you do, with your live-in dad, your famous stepmom, and your stupid dog, can we, Zack?"

Oh-kay. That was not the answer he'd expected. But Zack didn't say anything in reply. Neither did Malik.

Azalea stormed to the back of the bus and fiddled with her cell phone. She kept staring at the screen and, when she thought no one was looking, wiping her eyes.

Zack realized he was pretty lucky. Ever since Judy Magruder had come into his life, most of the sadness had gone out. The same couldn't be said for his two new friends. Malik's dad was out of work, his mom sick. Azalea looked like she'd just gotten some really bad news.

Uh-oh.

Her dad was in the army.

Soldiers sometimes got killed.

Maybe that was what her guardian ghost, Mary Jane Hopkins, had meant when she'd said, "She's in grave danger."

In danger of losing her father.

Between first and second periods, exploring a new shortcut, Zack heard piano music coming out of a classroom. It sounded so haunting he figured one of the guardian ghosts had learned to manipulate piano keys. So he followed the music to an empty classroom, where Azalea sat at a piano.

She saw Zack and immediately slammed the keyboard cover shut.

"What are you doing here?" she snapped at him.

"Nothing. I just heard the music. What was it?"

"Nothing. A song I made up."

"Really? Wow! That's incredible!"

"Yeah, right. Look, Zack, if you tell anybody . . ."

"I won't. I promise." He moved closer to the piano. "So, what's going on?"

"Huh?"

"Well, you've been acting kind of weird. . . ."

"Weird is what I do, Zack."

"I mean *weird* weird. What happened?"

She pried up the keyboard cover. Plunked a couple of sour notes.

"Oh, nothing. Just my dad almost got killed. Again."

"How?"

"A bullet. It killed his best buddy. Six inches to the left, it would've killed him."

"But he's okay?"

"Yeah. Well, this morning he's okay. Tonight, who knows? I don't want to lose my father, okay? I hardly even know the guy, he's gone so much."

Zack wondered if her dad's being in the army was why Azalea was so obsessed with death.

"It could happen any day, any second," she said softly.

Zack sat down. He could tell that Azalea needed to talk.

"I guess it's why I do the stupid Bloody Mary bit and visit graveyards and try to look like a vampire or a ghost. I want to believe in life after death, Zack."

He nodded.

"I want to believe that if . . . if the worst happens . . . that, I dunno, that somehow I could still maybe talk to my dad . . . tell him stuff. Crazy, huh?"

Zack thought long and hard before he spoke.

"You could," he said.

"What?"

"Your father's spirit won't die with his body."

"Right. Like you know."

"Azalea, I'm going to tell you something I've never told anybody, except my stepmom." He took a deep breath. "I see ghosts."

Azalea's raccoon eyes opened superwide.

"It's true. Honest. It started over the summer. Now, everywhere I look, I see them."

"Really?"

"Well, if they're there. This room is empty. Although at first I thought there might be one in here, a ghost who taught himself how to play the piano. . . ."

"Uh-huh."

"I didn't ask to be a ghost seer. It just sort of happened."

Azalea nodded. Very slowly.

"Yesterday, when I zoned out in the bathroom? I did see somebody in the mirror and her name, believe it or not, was Mary, but she wasn't Bloody Mary. . . ."

"Oh-kay. Thanks for sharing that with me, Zack. Good to know. Well, we better book. Don't want to be late for class."

"Are you feeling better?"

"Oh, I'm feeling fine, Zack. Just fine." She backed away from the piano bench toward the door. "See you in history class."

The way Azalea bolted out of the music room, Zack wasn't sure telling her the truth had been the smartest idea.

60

In history class, Ms. DuBois showed the class a picture of Horace P. Pettimore's headstone.

"This is his grave marker in the cemetery out back."

CAPTAIN HORACE PHINEAS PETTIMORE
1825–1900

．．—．．—．．—　—．．．．　．．———．．—．．　．．．———．．．

ALL THAT I HAVE
I LEAVE FOR HE
WHO COMES AFTER ME

．．—．．—．．—　—．．．．　．．———．．—．．　．．．———．．．

"What does it mean?" asked Benny.

"Well," said Ms. DuBois, "the eye floating above the inscription means he was a member of a group called the Freemasons. What about the epigraph? The bit between the decorative lines? The actual words?"

Zack did not raise his hand. He glanced at Malik. There was an anxious look on his friend's face. Maybe a wild glint in his eye. Wild? Malik? Impossible. Maybe he had gas.

186

But he was breathing kind of fast and sweating, too.

Then he started writing. Dots and dashes.

"I think," said Andrew Oldewurtel, a boy who always sat in the second row, behind Azalea, "that Mr. Pettimore is, like, you know, talking about how generous he was and how he left everything he had to us, the children who would, like, come after him, and how everything he did . . ."

While Andrew kept prattling, Malik kept writing.

Now letters under the dots and dashes.

"Interesting, Andrew," said Ms. DuBois. "Anyone else?"

"Well," said Sam Maroon, a guy whose guardian ghost used to play football back in the days when they didn't wear helmets, "I think . . ."

Zack didn't pay attention to what Sam Maroon thought.

While Ms. DuBois was looking the other way, Malik handed him a slip of paper.

"Those aren't 'decorative lines,'" Malik whispered. "It's Morse code. Think like a sailor! Like Captain Pettimore!"

Zack studied what Malik had written, ran the eraser end of his pencil along the line:

..._.. _._..   _ ....____ _._..   ... _ ___ _.. .

Zack realized that on the headstone, the lines above and below the letters were exactly the same.

..._.. _._..   _ ....____ _._..   ... _ ___ _.. .

He didn't know Morse code but Malik, of course, did.

In fact, he had it memorized, and this is what both lines said:

Find the second stone

Zack folded up the note so nobody else could see it. Malik was beaming.

They had found the "second stone," the doormat for the secret entrance to Horace Pettimore's treasure tunnel, the hiding place for his gold! That was why there was a huge hole in the foundation wall just above the stone! It was the gateway to riches.

And, of course, zombie hell.

Azalea was staring at the clock.

History class was almost over. They'd discussed Horace P. Pettimore's grave marker to death and talked about doing a cemetery crawl in a couple of weeks. Everybody applauded when Ms. DuBois gave Azalea credit for coming up with the idea. That was neat.

Then a couple of kids read their family tree reports out loud.

It was Malik's turn and it was cool to see how proud he was of the heroic ancestors he had discovered.

"And my great-grandfather from Alabama was one of the Tuskegee Airmen in World War II. . . ."

Finally, the bell rang.

Lunch was next, so everybody bolted for the door.

"I'll catch up with you guys in the cafeteria," Azalea said to Zack and Malik.

"Cool," said Zack.

Azalea waited for Zack and Malik and everybody else to leave the room.

Then she closed the door. Ms. DuBois looked up from her attendance book.

"What's wrong?"

Azalea took in a deep breath, because this was so not like her. She'd never had friends before. She'd never had to worry about them as much as she worried about her dad.

"Azalea?" Ms. DuBois prompted.

"Okay. Here's the thing. I'm worried about Zack."

"Really? Whatever for?"

"Ms. DuBois." Another deep breath. Then she just blurted it out. "This morning, Zack told me he can see dead people."

"Really? Like that boy in the movie?"

"I guess. He called himself a ghost seer. Claims he sees spirits everywhere. He even swears he actually saw Bloody Mary yesterday when we were goofing around in front of a bathroom mirror. Nobody ever sees Bloody Mary. They just freak themselves out because it's dark and I have a candle."

"A ghost seer?"

"That's what he called himself."

"Oh, my. And he's so young. . . ."

"Yeah. That was kind of my reaction, too."

Ms. DuBois nodded. "All right. Two things. First, you are to be commended for looking out for your friends. We could all learn from your example."

"Thanks, I guess. I sort of feel like I'm ratting him out."

"Nonsense. You are right to be concerned. Second, that cemetery crawl you suggested . . ."

"Yeah?"

"Let's do a trial run tomorrow, but with a small group. Say, you, me, Malik, and Zack. Perhaps being in the grave-yard, Zack will open up more about these spirits he thinks he sees and I'll be there to help him sort things out. They might just be figments of his imagination. His language arts instructor tells me Zack has a very vivid one."

"Well, his stepmom writes books about talking cats who go on vacation to Paris and junk."

"You see? Maybe he gets it from her. Anyway, we'll deal with it tomorrow. Will you tell Zack and Malik?"

Azalea nodded.

"Until then, don't say a word about Zack's 'special problem' to anyone else." Ms. DuBois had a far-off look in her eye. "I might need to bring a colleague with me tomorrow."

"A child psychologist or something?"

"No. Somebody else. Someone who's quite familiar with psychics and mediums and that sort of thing."

"Great."

Now Azalea felt better. She breathed a sigh of relief.

"Oh, I almost forgot. I found out the coolest thing last night," she said.

"What?"

"Well, I was working on my family tree, and my aunt Irene—that's who we're staying with—she tells me that she just found out from *her* mom that we're all related to a woman named Mary Jane Hopkins, who's like my great-great-great-great-great-great-great-great-grandmother or something. And guess what?"

"What?"

"This Mary Jane Hopkins—that's her married name—was Horace P. Pettimore's baby sister. So I'm related to the guy this whole school's named after! Isn't that awesome?"

Horace Pettimore's spirit raced up to the history classroom the instant he heard the name.

"This Mary Jane Hopkins—that's her married name—was Horace P. Pettimore's baby sister."

So.

Zachary Jennings wasn't the one.

It was the new girl.

Fine.

He could be a girl.

63

When Daphne DuBois was absolutely certain Azalea Torres was gone, she unlocked the bottom drawer of her filing cabinet and pulled out a rolled-up tube of paper.

She spread the wrinkled sheet on her desk, weighing down the four corners with a stapler, a tape dispenser, and two ceramic apples.

CHILD YOUNG SETH SEER GOLD

The words Madame Marie had scribbled while communicating with the ghost of John Lee Cooper practically leapt off the page.

CHILD YOUNG

Daphne had been quite clever, spending time socializing with the school's outcasts, the weaklings the popular kids picked on or simply ignored—the way she would have ignored them if she hadn't been desperate to find her own Seth Donnelly.

She needed, as her heroic ancestor had said from beyond the tomb, a ghost seer—the same phrase Zack Jennings had used to describe himself to his raccoon-faced girlfriend.

After weeks and weeks of work—pretending to be sweet, sitting every day at the nerd table, smelling miserably malodorous cafeteria food, feigning enjoyment of the company of the school's biggest losers—after a month of sheer hell, she had finally found her child.

Zack Jennings.

It made sense. Jennings was a sensitive sort. Always wasting his time worrying about others. Warped by a runaway imagination. Too compassionate, even to his dog.

She rolled the sketch paper back up. She returned it to the file drawer and pulled out the two small chalkboards sandwiched together, what the medium had called her spirit slates. She undid the strap.

During Madame Marie's séance, the spirit of John Lee Cooper had written a message inside the chalkboards, words that the medium herself never had the opportunity to read, since Eddie had killed her shortly after she'd come out of her trance.

FIND THE BOY
BEWARE THE GIRL

Daphne assumed that the girl was Azalea Torres. If, as she claimed, she was related to the Yankee scallywag

Captain Pettimore, she could prove problematic. No matter. Eddie would deal with Azalea. The ugly Goth girl would be dead before sundown on Saturday.

Daphne chuckled softly.

The thought of Azalea dead truly tickled her.

With all that ghastly makeup on her face, she looks half dead already.

Daphne needed to call her brother. Let him know they were a day away from redeeming their family's honor. A day away from reclaiming the Confederacy's gold.

She dug her cell phone out of her purse. Pressed speed dial number one.

Her brother answered on the first ring.

"Yes, boss. What's up?"

"Eddie, I found him!"

"Our ghost seer?"

"Yes. Young Zachary Jennings."

"Are you certain?"

"He confessed to a friend this morning. She, in turn, came to me."

"What if this Jennings boy is just making it up, calling himself a ghost seer to impress the girl?"

"I sense he is for real. He fits the profile. However, if it turns out he's lying, we'll kill him, just like we killed the dowser and Madame Marie."

"Good. When do we . . ."

"Tomorrow. I'm inviting Zack and two of his closest chums to come on a Saturday-morning field trip to the cemetery so he can receive further instructions from John Lee Cooper."

"This is wonderful news, Daphne. Must I keep pretending to be a janitor?"

"Yes. Just for one more day."

"All right. You're the boss. I'll catch up with you this afternoon. Seems Mr. Crumpler has another toilet for me to unplug."

"Eddie?"

"Yes, Daphne?"

"Generations of Coopers, the living and the dead, are very proud of us today."

"I know."

"One more thing: Tomorrow be sure to bring your pistol. And at least three bullets."

64

"McNulty! Come!"

The ghost of Horace Pettimore roused his zombie from his after-dinner nap. The creature was sprawled out on the padded lining torn from a cracked-open coffin. All that remained of the corpse he had been feasting on were a chauffeur's cap and a pair of wire-rimmed glasses.

"Prepare to move beyond the maze to your killing pit!"

"Yes, master."

"When the sun rises, my soul shall slip into its new body. I shall venture deep into the tunnels to reclaim my gold. Though you do not recognize me, you will obey me, the one who holds your soul, the one who carries the mark!"

"Yes, master."

"Move to your sentry post. Should any uninvited mortals follow the new me into the tunnels, destroy them!"

"Yes, master."

"Destroy and devour them!"

Now Daphne DuBois unlocked a second filing cabinet drawer.

She pulled out the bundle of musty old letters she had found in her grandmother's attic when she was a child.

The letters that had sent her and her brother on their lifelong quest to reclaim their family's honor.

And the Confederacy's stolen gold.

There was the original handwritten letter from John Lee Cooper, who had first tracked the villainous Captain Pettimore to North Chester, Connecticut, in 1873. Letters from other Coopers who had journeyed north from Georgia and Tennessee, seeking the gold.

And then there was *the* letter.

The one written on an old-fashioned typewriter by the hero teacher who, one hundred years earlier, had taught mathematics in that very room.

THE PETTIMORE SCHOOL FOR CHILDREN
Old Pike Road · North Chester · Connecticut

January 10, 1910

Dearest Grandmother Amanda:

I write you from the festering human cesspool of Connecticut, whose murdering sons killed so many of our brave soldiers during Mr. Lincoln's War of Northern Aggression.

As peculiar as this may sound, I bring you greetings from your beloved husband, my esteemed grandfather, the late John Lee Cooper, CSA.

Now, before you think me mad, consider how noble and strong your husband's spirit was in life. Know, then, that his soul lives on past death and that his spirit lingers in this realm, longing to finish the unresolved business of a life so villainously cut short by thieving Yankee devils.

Grandfather has found a way to communicate with me through the medium of a young boy named Seth Donnelly, one of my students. Having developed a certain confidence with the lad—a shy, sensitive type with one bully of a big brother, no other family, and no friends—I was not in the least bit surprised when he came to me claiming to be a "ghost seer" with a message from beyond the veil.

"The ghost of your grandfather, John Lee Cooper, told me where to find the entrance to Captain Pettimore's treasure tunnel."

The boy, who is also a member of the scouting group I chaperone, then showed me a rubbing he had made of the carvings in a most peculiar stone he had found where grandfather had sent him. To Seth, the angled scribbles above and below the single easily decipherable line held no meaning. I, however, immediately recognized them for what they were: a coded message. Having researched the dastardly captain's history prior to

moving here to become a teacher in the
same buildings where the vile beast
lived for so many years, having studied
grandfather's diary, I knew that Horace
P. Pettimore had been a Freemason long
before he became a powerful high priest
in the voodoo cult.

Oh, Grandmother Amanda, you should
have seen young Seth's eyes widen when I
told him the markings were a voodoo curse
scribbled by Captain Pettimore and meant
to harm small children, such as he and
his brother, if they dared look at the
stone a second time without an adult who
knew the chants required to shield them
from the witch doctor's "juju."

Meanwhile, I took the paper from the
lad and deciphered the secret message.

I now know where the entrance to
Pettimore's treasure tunnel is located.
I have no fear of the "zombie" he so
brazenly claims guards his gold, as
I know it is simply another of the
villain's heinous lies, meant to scare
off any honorable sons of the South brave
enough to venture into the labyrinth to
reclaim what is rightfully ours.

Tomorrow, dearest Grandmother, I will

secure the stolen gold and redeem our
family's good name.

Of course, I will need to dispose of
Seth Donnelly, and his brother, Joseph,
as well, for I fear that those two share
secrets.

'I will have Seth lead Joseph and me to
the spot where the stone and tunnel
entrance are located. I will then execute
them both in the most merciful fashion, a
single bullet to their heads. I will do
this late at night, when the school is
deserted, so I might drag their bodies
back to the building and, in a cramped
corridor I know of, start a fire that
will consume both their bodies and melt
the lead bullets nestled inside their
skulls. I will make the whole thing look
like a tragic accident brought on by the
boys' own careless acts and will appear
to have attempted a dramatic rescue
before escaping from the blaze out my
classroom window.

Next week, or perhaps next month, I
will resign my position at the school,
claiming to be overwrought with grief
from the death of my two "precious
charges," and return to Georgia with our
gold. The South shall rise again!

Be well, Grandmother.

Know that your husband's work, thanks
in no small measure to his own indomitable
spirit, finally nears its completion.

Give Louella my love and kiss my
babies for me. Tell them my mission in
the godforsaken land of the Connecticut
Yankee demons nears its completion and I
will soon return home to the bosom of my
family.

> Faithfully yours,
> your loving grandson,
>
> *Patrick J. Cooper*

Lunch wasn't much fun for Zack on Friday.

The two tables had grown to three, but Zack was worried about Malik, who had brought his calculator to the cafeteria and kept crunching numbers instead of munching his food.

"What're you working on?" Zack asked.

"Hmm? Oh, this? It's nothing."

"Then why are you working on it?"

Malik blinked about a hundred times. "Just for fun."

Azalea wasn't there for a snappy comeback. She was six or seven chairs away, over at table three with Benny, who hadn't even asked Zack today what he was going to blow up next.

So Zack ate his PB and J in silence.

Finally, Ms. DuBois—who was like twenty minutes late—came to the table. She sat down directly across from Zack, in the seat where Azalea usually sat.

"Sorry I'm late. Mr. Crumpler has me filling out more forms. Stop by this afternoon and we'll finalize our plans for the trial-run field trip tomorrow."

"Cool, can I come?" asked a boy named Riley Mack, whose guardian ghost was, believe it or not, a German shepherd named Thor. He'd been the family pet. Died the year before. Riley was his favorite. Used to sneak Thor a hamburger whenever the family cooked out.

The dog didn't tell Zack all this. It was more like telepathy or something.

"I'm afraid tomorrow's field trip isn't for everyone, Riley," said Ms. DuBois, her voice dripping with honey. "It's something of a practice. Zack, Malik, Azalea, and I shall be the guinea pigs. If our adventure proves fun and educational, we'll still take the whole class the weekend before Halloween!"

"Awesome," said Riley.

"What time shall I pick you up tomorrow?" Ms. DuBois asked Zack.

"That's okay. My mom and dad can drop me off."

"Don't be silly. I drive right past your house anyway. Shall we say nine a.m.?"

"Okay."

"Um, I don't need a ride tomorrow," said Malik. "I'm gonna bike it."

"Very well. How about you, Azalea?"

"Sure. Nine will be fine."

Okay, that was extremely weird.

Not only did it rhyme, but just the day before, Azalea had told Zack she never, ever woke up before noon on Saturday or Sunday!

"I saw Captain Pettimore," Joseph said to Seth.

"Where?"

"Drifting through the tunnels. I asked him, 'How's tricks?' and he says he's shoving off in the morning. Returning to the distant shore."

"Can he do that?" asked Seth.

"Maybe. Remember, kiddo, he's always boasting about being a big-cheese voodoo king. Says he can do all sorts of neat tricks we can't."

"Mr. Cooper told me Pettimore was a witch doctor— back when I found the stone."

"Yeah, well, the captain says he found himself a new 'earthen vessel' and will be coming back down tomorrow to fetch his gold."

"You know what that means?" said Seth, his eyes widening.

"Yep." Joseph's smile grew so wide his teeth ran from ear to ear. "Some other folks will see what he's up to and come down here after him! Adult folks!"

"So we can leave here, too!"

"Hold your horses, little brother. First we need to set things right. Undo the wrong done to us!"

"Will killing an adult set us free, Joseph?"

"Maybe. I think so. And if killing one grown-up don't make me feel better about moving on, well, by gum, we'll find us another one to lock inside that smoky box! And if that don't work, we'll keep killin' 'em till I say we've killed enough!"

Seth just nodded. He always did what his big brother told him to.

"Where's your zombie?"

The creature loped out of the darkness, his arms flopping limply, his knuckles nearly scraping the floor.

"Tell him to stoke the furnace," said Joseph.

"Stoke the furnace."

"Yes, master."

"We need it smokin' by morning! Go on. Tell him!"

"We need it smokin' by morning."

"Yes, master." Seth's zombie hobbled over to the woodpile, pried a log free, carried it to the furnace, and jammed it into the first firebox.

Then he repeated the trek a dozen or more times while Joseph broke out in song.

Glory, glory, hallelujah
Teacher hit us with a ruler
He shot us in the head
To make certain we was dead
But now we're killin' them!

Seth, on the other hand, didn't feel much like singing.

207

When the final bell rang, Zack hit the halls, looking for Malik, because they usually rode the bus home together.

Couldn't find him.

So he looked around for Azalea.

Couldn't find her, either.

He stuck his head into Ms. DuBois's room. She was at her desk, rummaging through a stack of yellowed envelopes.

"Hi," he said.

"Whaaa?" Her knees banged the bottom of her desk when she nearly jumped out of her seat.

"Sorry. Didn't mean to startle you."

Ms. DuBois touched her hair. Adjusted her blouse. "Can I help you with something, Zack?"

"I was kind of looking for Azalea and Malik."

"Sorry. I haven't seen them." Now the teacher narrowed her eyes and gave Zack the most peculiar look. It reminded Zack of the way ladies at the supermarket study a piece of fruit they want to thump to see if it's fresh. "Have you seen anyone *else* today, Zack?"

"Sure. Lots of people."

"Any, perhaps, that I did not, or, more specifically, *could* not see?"

Zack had no idea what Ms. DuBois was talking about or why her sky blue eyes suddenly looked like they had thunderclouds in them.

"Um, I don't think so. . . ."

Ms. DuBois's bright red lips curled up into a grin. "No. Of course not. Silly me for asking." Then she winked.

"Oh-kay, then. See you tomorrow, Ms. DuBois."

"Yes. Nine a.m. Sharp. Your house. I'll toot my horn."

"Right."

And Zack walked out the door, wondering if the field trip to the Civil War cemetery was really such a hot idea.

By the time he got to his locker, the hallways were empty. He'd have to hurry to catch the last bus home.

When he popped up the latch, there was Mr. Willoughby.

"Good afternoon, Zachary."

"Hi." Zack grabbed his jacket and backpack. "Sorry, can't really chat right now. I'm late for the bus. . . ."

"Indeed, well, I suppose this can wait . . . well, no, actually it can't. . . ."

"What is it now?" said Zack, somewhat sarcastically. "Are the two zombies on the prowl all of a sudden?"

"Well, now that you mention it, yes."

"What?"

"The game's afoot!"

"Huh?"

"Er, the troops are on the move?"

And then the most bizarre thing happened: Mr. Willoughby turned into Mary Jane Hopkins.

"Stop him! Stop him!"

"Who?"

"My brother! Captain Pettimore! He is coming for—"

Zack didn't get to hear the rest.

Someone grabbed him by the collar and yanked him away from the locker.

"Who you talking to, wacko?"

Kurt Snertz stood in front of his three toughest friends.

"Where are all your little buddies? All those nerds from the nerd table?"

"Guess they went home."

"Yeah," said Kurt. "And you know what else?"

"What?"

"The teachers go home fast on Fridays, too. Looks like you and me are finally all alone."

"What about these other guys?"

Kurt's brow knitted in confusion. "Huh?"

"Your three friends. We can't be alone if they're here."

Zack heard a laugh. And it didn't come from Kurt or the three goons.

Wherever it came from, the laugh kept Zack feeling brave.

"I mean, how can we ever be alone, Kurt, if you always need three or four guys to make you feel tough?"

Another laugh. Someone different.

"See, 'alone' would mean just you and me. So if you

were, I don't know, waiting until we were alone to ask me to dance or something . . ."

A gale of laughs greeted that line.

"Shut up!" said Kurt.

And then Zack saw who was doing all the laughing: A whole host of guardian ghosts materialized in the hallway, at least two dozen of them. All the spirits he had done favors for had clustered together to become his cheering section.

Zack felt bold.

Kurt balled up his fist.

"Wait for it," said the ghost who used to play football without a helmet. From the looks of his bent nose, he also used to box without a face mask.

So Zack stood in front of his locker and waited.

Snertz's face turned purple.

"I'm gonna cream you, Jennings!"

"Wait for it!" the ghost coached from the wings.

Zack stood stock-still.

Snertz cocked back his arm.

"Aaaaaaand . . . duck!" the ghost said.

Zack ducked.

Snertz's fist smashed into the locker's steel door.

"Ooowwwwww!!!"

The ghosts applauded.

"Well played!" "Good ducking!" "Nicely done, Zack!"

And now the laughs were coming from Kurt's friends, too.

Kurt kept shaking out his fist, trying to make the pain go away.

Zack casually strolled toward the exit. The guardian ghosts escorted him down the hall.

Behind him, he could hear Kurt Snertz bellowing at his bullies.

"Shut up, you guys! Quit laughing!"

"But," said one of them, "it's funny, man. When you slugged that door, you dented it!"

"Shut up!" And then Snertz started screaming at Zack. "You're dead, Jennings! You hear me? Dead!"

Zack didn't look back. He calmly stepped outside and, when he saw the last bus home to Stonebriar Road, said a quick thanks to his ghost pals.

Then he ran faster than he had run when he'd snuck Zipper out of the building.

Because if he missed the last bus, Snertz's prediction would undoubtedly come true: Zack Jennings would be a dead man.

"Sounds like fun," Zack's dad said when he heard about the Saturday-morning history crawl through the old cemetery. "Can Judy and I tag along?"

They were sitting around the dinner table, eating fried chicken. Judy didn't cook it. The Colonel did.

"That would be fun," said Judy. "You guys need extra adults?"

"Not really. Ms. DuBois wants to keep this first trip small. Just me, Azalea, Malik, and her. She probably thinks it might get boring, just looking at gravestones and junk."

"Boring?" said his dad. "Maybe some of the spirits will rise up out of their graves and wail at you for cutting across their lawns! Moo-ha-ha!"

Both Zack and Judy pretended to find that funny. Gave him a weak "heh-heh-ha"-style laugh.

Poor Dad. He didn't have a clue.

After dinner, Zack and Zipper were playing fetch in the backyard.

That was when Davy showed up.

"Howdy, pardner. Hey there, Zip!"

Zipper wagged his tail. Davy was probably his second-favorite boy in the world, even though Davy was from some otherworldly world.

"So, Davy, what's going on?" Zack asked. "Mr. Willoughby started babbling in my locker and then Mary Jane Hopkins took his place and then Kurt Snertz . . ."

"Yep. Things are all in a jumble. But you were smart not to invite your pops and Judy to join you tomorrow. . . ."

"Well, Ms. DuBois . . ."

"Pardner?"

"Yeah?"

"We need to have us a little chat about Ms. Daphne DuBois."

Zack nodded. "She had a real peculiar look on her face this afternoon."

"Boy, howdy, did she ever."

"You saw it?"

"Yep. Folks upstairs asked me to keep an eye on Ms. D today."

"And?"

"Zack, let's just say you can't judge a book by its cover, especially if it's a phony one."

"Really? But she seems so nice. . . ."

"Yep, she sure *seems* that way, don't she? She wants you to lead her to some kind of treasure tunnel. Don't do it, hear?"

"Don't worry. That's where the zombie is. Said so on the warning stone!"

"That's the other thing I need to talk to you about."

"The zombies?"

"Yep. Like I said before, we can't see much of what they're up to, on account of all the voodoo hoodoo spells, but at least one of them zombies started movin' around today, goin' places he ain't been in years."

"Is it looking for children's brains to eat?"

"Maybe. Can't say for sure. Wouldn't doubt it. This particular zombie feller is the fiercest, most vicious creature Captain Pettimore shipped up here from Louisiana. Tall, bone-thin man with a dinosaur-style head, all jaws and teeth and eyeballs buggier than a bullfrog's."

Zack tried not to picture this beast while Davy kept describing him.

"On the hunt, he moves fast—like a two-legged cheetah. He can rip off your head and crack open your skull, lickety-split."

Zack struggled to find his voice. "You can kill a zombie with fire, though, right? I read that in a book. It was a comic book, but . . ."

"Yep. Fire's just about the only way to stop a zombie."

"Just about?"

"Yep."

"Is there another way?"

Davy looked around the backyard. "Well, maybe . . ."

Thunder rumbled across the cloudless sky.

Davy mumbled, "Dadgummit," under his breath and quit talking.

Zack had already gotten into enough trouble with fire

over the summer; he didn't want to use it again if he didn't have to. "If there's some other way to stop this thing . . ."

Davy looked squirmy. He glanced up at the sky. "Zack, you know I can't come right out and tell you what to do."

Zack couldn't believe this. "Because of the stupid rules?"

"Yep."

"You've got an indestructible zombie with ginormous fangs and superhuman strength who could devour a whole school full of kids first thing Monday morning and you won't tell me how to stop him without burning down the building?"

"Can't, I reckon."

Zack more or less pouted for a second. "Stupid rules," he grumbled.

Zipper groaned in agreement.

"Well, I best be goin'. . . ."

Davy started to fade away.

"Wait!" Zack pleaded. "Don't go! Not without telling me!"

Oddly, Davy lifted a foot, examined the bottom of his shoe.

"What are you doing?"

"I got me a hole in my . . . what do you call that thing?"

"Your shoe?"

"On the bottom there."

"Your sole?"

Davy touched his nose. Held up two fingers.

"I have to guess a second word?"

Davy nodded.

Man! He couldn't tell Zack how to stop the zombie but he had time to play charades?

"Dang, I like pickles because they come in a . . ."

"Sandwich?"

"Think glass, pardner."

"A jar?"

Davy touched his nose again. Gestured for Zack to butt the two words up against each other.

"Sole. Jar."

"Hey, that sounds like a dadburn plan!"

"What? Wait a second. Are you trying to tell me I need to find the zombies' soul jars to stop them?"

"Shoot, pardner. I ain't tellin' you nothin'. That'd be against the rules."

And with a wink, Davy was gone.

71

At 9:01 on Saturday morning, Zack heard a car tooting its horn in the driveway.

"There's Ms. DuBois," said Judy, waving out the window. "You all set, Zack?"

"Yeah."

"She seems like a terrific teacher," said his dad.

Yeah, she sure seems that way, Zack wanted to say just like Davy had said it. But for reasons still not clear, he was supposed to keep his mom, his dad, and all other adults out of this.

"Have fun," said his dad.

"Come on," said Judy. "I'll walk you to the car."

They went out the front door. Zipper followed.

"Well, hello again, Mrs. Jennings!" Ms. DuBois called out the driver's-side window. Zack could see Azalea in the backseat. She looked kind of sleepy.

"This is such a neat idea," Judy said. "Are you going to do headstone rubbings?"

"We surely are," gushed Ms. DuBois. "I packed butcher paper and a box of black crayons."

"Do one for me, okay, Zack?"

"Sure, Mom."

"Good morning, Azalea," Judy called into the backseat.

Azalea opened an eye. "Good morning to you, too, ma'am."

"Well, we best be going," Ms. DuBois said very quickly. "Malik is meeting us at the school."

"Okay," said Zack.

Zipper grumbled.

Zack got a screwy idea. Zipper had been pretty helpful in the past when Zack had had to deal with demons. And since Zack had no idea what he was getting into . . .

"Can I bring my dog?"

Now Ms. DuBois blinked like a broken stoplight. "Pardon?"

"Saturday's usually the day I spend a ton of time with Zipper. . . ."

"Fine," said Ms. DuBois, obviously in a rush. "Bring your dog. It'll be fun."

"Cool. See ya, Mom."

Judy looked a little puzzled.

"Um, okay . . ."

Zack wished he could tell her what was going on.

Then again, he didn't really know.

Just that Ms. DuBois was a book with a phony cover and there were two zombies moving around underneath the school, but you could kill them with fire or if you opened up their soul jars, something Zack had researched on the Internet after playing backyard guessing games with Davy the night before, and Azalea was in some sort of grave danger and Zack was going to spend the day rubbing tombstones. Other than that, it was just your typical, normal Saturday.

The car pulled into the street.

"Finally!" said Azalea. "Who was that woman anyway?"

Okay. Azalea wasn't very normal, either.

For whatever reason, when Zack, Zipper, Azalea, and Ms. DuBois walked into the school, the new janitor was in the lobby waiting for them.

"Good morning, Eddie," said Ms. DuBois.

"Good mornin', Daphne. You brought a dog?"

The janitor was apparently off duty. He was wearing khaki pants and a golf jacket instead of his usual green work clothes.

"Zack insisted."

"Very well. Shouldn't pose a problem." The janitor tapped a bulge in the chest of his jacket. Zack didn't like it when he did that. He watched a lot of movies. Jacket bulges, especially when tapped, usually meant hidden guns and shoulder holsters.

All of a sudden, Zack remembered the pair of ghosts who had been trailing the janitor down the hall: They'd both had bullet holes in their heads!

"Why's the janitor here?" he asked.

"Oh, he's an expert on graveyards," said Ms. DuBois.

Yeah—putting people into them, Zack thought.

"Has Malik arrived?" she asked.

"Nope," said Eddie. "But Mr. Sherman, the boy's father, he swung by about five minutes ago."

"My goodness. What did *he* want?"

"Well, the poor man says he cannot for the life of him find his son. Thought maybe he came over here. Seems they had a big fight last night. Something to do with money. Mr. Sherman kept mumbling how it was all his fault. . . ."

"Malik ran away from home?"

"So it would seem."

Now Zack saw somebody nobody else (other than Zipper) could see: an African American man dressed in a World War II aviator uniform. Helmet on. Goggles up. Zack squinted so he could read the name patch sewn to his flight jacket: SHERMAN.

Malik's guardian ghost! Probably his great-granddad, the one who'd flown fighter planes with the Tuskegee Airmen.

While Ms. DuBois and the janitor kept jabbering, Zack casually strolled across the lobby and pretended to be interested in the baseball trophies on display in a glass case.

Because Mr. Sherman was standing inside it.

"You're Zack?" the airman asked.

He nodded.

"Malik's in trouble."

Zack raised his eyebrows.

"He went through that hole you boys found. He's

looking for the treasure. Wants to sell the gold and buy his mom the medicine she needs." The airman shook his head. "Bravest and craziest thing the boy's ever done. Sure his heart's in the right place, but he isn't using his head. You have to go get him, Zack. Malik doesn't stand a chance down there on his own. Who knows what he'll run into?"

Oh, Zack had a pretty good idea: *a brains-eating zombie!*

"And, whatever you do, don't tell those two where Malik is." Airman Sherman gestured toward Ms. DuBois and Eddie, the janitor. "They are not to be trusted. It's up to you, Zack. Are you going to go down there and help Malik?"

"Zack?" said Ms. DuBois.

"Are you ready to go, son?" asked the janitor.

Zack was facing Mr. Sherman when he answered.

"Yes, sir. I am."

He was also ready not to believe another word Ms. DuBois or Eddie, the pistol-packing janitor, had to say.

73

Kurt Snertz lowered the binoculars.

He was lying on his stomach, spying on Zack Jennings, his stupid little dog, the new history teacher, and the bizarro Goth chick Azalea Torres. Snertz's right fist was wrapped in a bandage; he had sprained it slugging the locker.

Today Jennings would pay for that. Maybe his mangy mutt, too!

Snertz watched his targets march into the school.

He lost visual contact.

"Darn it!"

He'd been tailing the Jennings wimp since first thing that morning. So far, he'd seen the dork and his dad take their stupid dog out for a stupid walk and then go home to eat what looked like stupid pancakes.

Now he was with a stupid teacher.

Kurt would have to bide his time. Catch Jennings when he wasn't being protected.

"Soon," he muttered to himself. "Soon!"

Then he crawled closer to the school.

74

Malik, holding a flashlight, stood frozen in fear at the top of a steep staircase.

The monster, crouching at the bottom in a dimly lit pit, glared up at him with burning red eyes. A deep, throaty purr rumbled up the steps.

Some kind of dog, Malik thought. *It has to be some kind of mutant dog.* It was the only logical explanation.

Then he remembered the first line of code carved into the stone he and Zack had found in the janitor's closet: *A zombie guards my treasure well.*

The first time Malik had read it, he had focused on the treasure bit. Now he was thinking about zombies. Corpses brought back to life by powerful voodoo sorcerers to do their masters' bidding. Reanimated dead people that feasted on human flesh and brains.

If you wanted to guard millions of dollars' worth of gold, a zombie would sure make a good watchdog.

He inched his gaze down a bit. In the jittering circle of light twenty feet below, he saw slick fangs glistening with slime.

"W-what are you?" Malik stammered.

The beast rumbled up another purr.

"Stay away!" Malik shouted, wishing he'd spent more time playing video games instead of reading books, because there were all sorts of ways to kill zombies in video games. He'd heard guys talking about it on the bus.

"Leave me alone! Go! Get out of here!"

Then, much to Malik's surprise, the creature turned and scurried off into the darkness.

Still terrified, Malik stepped backward into the tunnel that had brought him down to this split and the two staircases. There was probably some other kind of monster waiting at the bottom of the other set of steps. He swung his flashlight left to check it out and the beam bounced off tiny circles of glass.

Antique pocket watches suspended from tarnished brass hooks on a wall between the two staircases.

Malik counted thirty-nine. They seemed to be clustered in groupings. Two watches. Three. Two.

Like letters in words.

Another code! he thought.

"The watches tell you which way to go," Malik mumbled out loud. "How to avoid the zombie!"

Could the arrows on the hour and minute hands be pointing in the direction he should head to stay safe?

No. They were pointing up, down, sideways—all over the place.

He studied the thirty-nine clock faces hanging on the far wall.

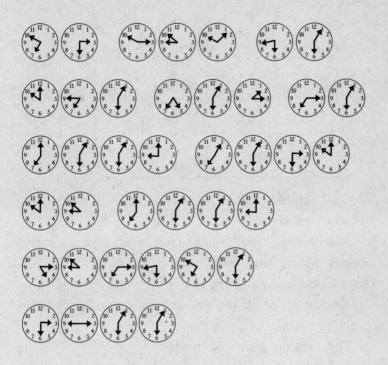

It looked like the dials on a water meter.
But it was something else. A secret message.
It had to be.
Now all Malik had to do was figure out what it said.

It was Saturday and Benny was bored.

So he biked over to Zack's house.

Maybe they could blow something up out in the woods. Maybe they could stick a firecracker in an old Lego model and watch the bricks fly.

Benny hopped off his bike and ran up to Zack's front porch to ring the bell.

His stepmom answered the door.

"Hi, Mrs. Jennings!"

"Hi, Benny."

"Can Zack come out and play?"

"Well, he's not here right now. . . ."

"Oh."

"He had to go to school."

"Really? On a Saturday?"

Mrs. Jennings nodded. "It's something, uh, special."

"Yeah?"

"I'm sure he wishes you were there with him . . . but, well, this is more or less a dry run . . . a test."

"He's testing something?"

"Yeah. More or less."

"Okay. Thanks, Mrs. Jennings."

"Sure, Benny. Say hi to your mom and dad for me."

"Okay."

She went back into the house.

Benny grabbed his bike.

This is so awesome! he thought. Zack was definitely doing something major at the school. Even if it was only a dry run or a test, it'd be exciting.

He pedaled hard.

He had to be there to see it.

He saw his buddy Andrew Oldewurtel riding around in circles on his bike in the street in front of his house.

"Hey, Andrew!"

"Hey, Benny. Where you goin'?"

"School. Zack's gonna do something amazing!"

"When?"

"Like right now!"

"Awesome! Did you tell Riley and Emily?"

"No time," said Benny, biking up the street.

"I'll text them," shouted Andrew. "They can text Jessie and Harry and Laurel. Hang on. I'm right behind you, man!"

Zack, Zipper, and Azalea followed Ms. DuBois and the janitor out the front door of the school.

Zack wished he didn't have to keep pretending to be interested in the cemetery crawl. It had been Azalea's big idea and she didn't seem interested in it at all. She had barely said a word to anybody all day. She didn't seem herself.

Zack needed to be downstairs. He needed to crawl through the hole in the old root cellar wall and find Malik. Given the way Azalea had been acting, he couldn't ask her for help. And he definitely couldn't ask Ms. DuBois or Eddie!

"Um, where are we going?" Zack asked.

"The graveyard, Zack," said Ms. DuBois. "Where else would we do a cemetery crawl? Now, I thought we'd start our field trip with one of the oldest headstones. The marker commemorating the valiant John Lee Cooper."

"Have fun," said Azalea. "I'm heading inside."

"What?" said Ms. DuBois. "Are you feeling okay, Azalea?"

"Fit as a fiddle. I just forgot to use the latrine this morning."

Ms. DuBois sighed. "Fine. But hurry. Meet us down by the river at Colonel Cooper's headstone."

"Right. Will do." Azalea went back into the school.

"Come along, Zachary," said the janitor, who had an extremely eerie smile plastered on his face. "We mustn't keep the colonel waiting."

Zack and Zipper followed the two adults up a narrow footpath through the forest behind the gymnasium.

Zipper whimpered. Used his snout to nudge Zack's ankle.

When Zack looked down, he saw the lacy hem of a Civil War–era wedding gown: Mary Jane Hopkins was walking beside them, her body passing straight through trees and boulders blocking her path.

"He has her!" she gasped. "Captain Pettimore has taken over Azalea's body. He will use her to retrieve his gold and then snuff out her soul. You have to save her, Zack! You have to force my brother's spirit to leave Azalea's body before her own soul withers away into nothingness!"

Zack nodded.

He'd just add it to his list.

Mary Jane Hopkins disappeared.

"This footpath will take us to the cemetery road," said Ms. DuBois. "But I'm sure you already knew that, Zack.

I'm sure you sneak over this way all the time, to chat with your friends."

"Not really. Mostly we hang out in the cafeteria or at my house after school. . . ."

"I meant your *other* friends."

"Huh?"

"We are given to understand," said Eddie, "that you, Zachary Jennings, are conversant with those on the distant shore."

"You mean like over in France?"

"Ghosts," said Ms. DuBois, rather nastily. "You talk to ghosts! Don't try to deny it. Azalea told me!"

"What? She was just kidding. She made it up!"

Eddie pulled out a pistol with a wooden handle, a brass trigger guard, and a very long barrel.

"You better be able to talk to ghosts, son," he said. "Or you know what?"

"What?"

"I will most assuredly turn you into one."

77

Judy and George sat in the TV room.

George flipped through sixteen channels, then paused on a college football game before clicking forward another sixteen channels.

He handed the remote to Judy who flipped back through thirty-two channels.

"I miss Zack and Zipper," she said.

"Me too," said George.

"You want to take them lunch?"

"Yeah. We could pick up a couple pizzas. Swing by the cemetery. Surprise everybody!"

"Excellent!" Judy zapped off the TV. "But no pepperoni for Zipper."

"Right. No pepperoni for the dog."

"He gets gassy, George."

"I know. Besides, he prefers sausage."

Judy laughed and scooped up her keys.

This would be fun! A pizza picnic and maybe she could do her own grave rubbing. Later they'd take the kids to the Olde Mill for cold cider and hot doughnuts.

It'd be a perfect October Saturday!

78

It was incredible!

Daphne DuBois stood beside the grave of John Lee Cooper, marveling at Zack Jennings as the young ghost seer, like Seth Donnelly before him, conversed with her deceased ancestor—the first Southerner to come north to retrieve the Confederacy's stolen gold.

Bringing the boy's dog along for the field trip turned out to be an excellent idea.

The dog could see ghosts, too!

Daphne DuBois could tell, just by studying the angle of the dog's unblinking stare, that the spirit of John Lee Cooper was standing in front of his headstone.

"I understand," Zack said to the empty air.

Then, of course, there was a pause as John Lee Cooper spoke to the boy.

"Yes, sir. I'll show them where Captain Pettimore put his special marker."

This was amazing!

"You say there are no more booby traps in the tunnels? No more guards?"

Of course not, Daphne thought. Pettimore had died a century earlier. Any guards he had hired had long since abandoned their posts.

"What? The message on the stone is written in code? Can you tell me how to crack it? Good. Thank you, sir."

Daphne looked at her brother, Eddie. He still had the .44-caliber Colt revolver aimed at Zack.

"Oh, put that thing away, Edward! Zack's doing exactly what we told him to do." Then she whispered, "I think he has a crush on me. I think all the boys do."

Eddie lowered the gun, moved closer.

"But what about the girl?" he whispered.

Right.

She had nearly forgotten. The warning scribbled on Madame Marie's spirit slates: *Find the boy. Beware the girl.*

"Hurry back to the school," she said to her brother. "Find Azalea. Put her out of *our* misery."

Eddie smiled. "One lead ball to the head is all it should take!"

Edward Cooper DuBois?" the ghost snarled. "You come back here with that pistol!"

"Yes," said Zack. "I understand."

"Consarn it all! Tell him to turn around, boy!"

John Lee Cooper was probably the angriest, most spiteful, meanest-tempered ghost Zack had ever encountered, a sour-faced man with a long, curly beard, a bird beak for a nose, and two tiny black eyes.

"Boy, you tell Edward Cooper DuBois to come back here and put a bullet in your fool brain!"

Zack nodded. "So all we need to know is how to convert Roman numerals to crack the code?"

"What? I didn't say that. Consarn it, boy! You've not spoke one true word of what I told you! Tell Daphne she must be careful. There be a ferocious voodoo zombie standing guard in that tunnel."

"And once we find the stone, we have nothing to worry about?"

"Why, you little Yankee coot! Where's that Donnelly boy? Him I could talk to. You're nothin' but a sockdologizing young whippersnapper!"

"Thank you, sir. Is that everything?"

"No, dagnabit! There's booby traps and danger around every corner! Captain Pettimore was clever and cunning! Spent years building his fortifications. You go down the wrong tunnel, the wrong staircase, that zombie of his will rip the flesh right off your bones!"

"Okay. Thanks. Hope to talk to you again soon, sir."

Zack turned away from the headstone and snicked his tongue so Zipper would quit staring at the ghost, too.

Zipper turned toward the teacher.

"Consarn it! Don't you turn your back on me, boy. I'll knock you into a cocked hat, you no-account hornswoggler!"

Zack smiled at Ms. DuBois. Zipper wagged his tail.

"All set? I know where we need to go."

Malik stood in the tunnel, studying the faces of the pocket watches.

He'd been working on the puzzle for quite some time and still hadn't cracked the code.

He had assumed that it was a number/letter cipher, as in A=1, B=2, and so forth. Or Z=1, Y=2, and backward. But only a few of the watches were set precisely on the hour. So that wouldn't work.

He focused on what had to be a four-letter word.

"Seven, six-oh-five, six-oh-five, nine."

The two letters in the middle were definitely the same. Probably "e," one of the most commonly occurring letters in the English language. Malik figured it was a vowel, because the repeated letter was in the middle of the word. The letters at the front and back of the word were different.

"So it might be 'deer' but it can't be 'peep.' Though, it could be 'beep' . . . 'keep' . . . 'deep.'"

Next Malik tried adding the numbers together if the time shown wasn't a straight-up hour. So 6:05 became six plus one—seven. *Or should it be six plus five—eleven?*

Malik stopped thinking when he heard somebody coming!

He doused his flashlight, huddled up against the wall between support beams.

"McNulty? Stand down. It's me!"

It sounded like Azalea, only different. Gruff.

Somebody holding a lantern came marching down the long mine shaft that led from the root cellar to the wall with all the watches.

Malik peeked around a post.

It *was* Azalea! Only it wasn't. Something was different.

She passed Malik. He couldn't see what she was doing. Didn't dare lean forward again. She was too close.

"Right," he heard her say. "McNulty? It's me! Your captain! I'm coming down."

Malik waited another minute. Then he started breathing again. He stepped forward. Azalea was gone but Malik couldn't tell which staircase she had chosen when she'd reached the split.

She'd called herself the captain.

Malik shone his flashlight on the wall of watches.

He remembered the final lines from the warning stone:

Next stand watch like a sailor should and your prospects shall be very good.

"Stand watch like a sailor should."

Clever. Even used the word "watch." The old code was there to help him crack this new one.

It was definitely time to start thinking like a sailor again!

81

"Horace P. Pettimore wrote a secret message on the cornerstone of the school building!" Zack said to Ms. DuBois.

"Of course! Excellent!"

She was walking so fast Zack and Zipper had to trot to keep up.

"But," said Zack, "Colonel Cooper didn't tell me which corner."

His string of lies to Ms. DuBois was all part of his plan to stall the history teacher until . . . well, until he came up with a better plan!

Fortunately, Pettimore Middle School had been added on to so many times it had a billion corners. It might take hours to find the corner of the foundation where the Masons had laid the ceremonial stone.

"So," Zack said, "why don't you and Eddie search the north and south sides of the building? Azalea and I can check out the east and west . . ."

And I'll run downstairs to rescue Malik!

"No need for us to split up, Zack," said Ms. DuBois. "I found the cornerstone my first day on the job. I had a hunch that since Captain Pettimore had been a Mason, he may have had his 'brother Masons' place a secret message there! This way!"

The wording on the cornerstone was brief and to the point:

MDCCCXCV
LAID BY THE MASONIC FRATERNITY
SO ALL MAY FIND THE KNOWLEDGE
WHICH THEY SEEK

"There you are!" Eddie came around the corner of the main building, tucking the long barrel of his pistol into his pants. "Sadly, I could not find Miss Torres."

"No matter. We'll deal with her later. Quickly, Mr. Jennings! Decode the inscription!"

"Well, uh . . . this might take a while. . . ."

"Nonsense. The ghost of Colonel Cooper told you precisely what to do!"

"Riiight. Okay. Well . . . uh . . . the trick is in the Roman numerals there."

"Of course! MDCCCXCV! What does it mean?"

"Eighteen ninety-five."

"We know that," said Eddie. "What else?"

"Well . . . and this is what he told me . . . he said . . . um . . . each letter stands for a word . . ."

"Yes?" said Ms. DuBois eagerly.

"M . . . D . . . that could be 'My Dog' . . ."

Zipper barked.

"Or 'Medical Doctor' . . ."

"Didn't Colonel Cooper tell you precisely what words the letters stood for?" demanded Ms. DuBois, who didn't smell much like warm cinnamon rolls anymore. More like boiled cabbage.

"Yes, yes. He did. But you guys are screaming and hollering at me so much and you've got a pistol tucked into your pants so I'm kind of nervous and when I get nervous I forget stuff. Maybe we should go back to the graveyard and . . ."

Eddie raised his pistol. Cocked back the brass hammer. Pointed the slender steel barrel directly between Zack's eyes.

"Would you like to start talking to ghosts the easy way, son?"

"No, sir."

"Then tell us where to find the gold!"

Zack stared at the letters.

"Miles . . . Down . . . Connecticut . . . Country . . . Christmas . . ."

"There you guys are!"

Eddie quickly hid the pistol under his jacket.

It was Benny.

"We heard Zipper's bark! Figured you guys were back here. What's going on?"

Benny was with Andrew, Chuck, Alyssa, Harry, Jessie, Ryan, Amanda, Joseph Stockli, Laurel Jumper, Riley Mack, Marty Tappan, Rachel Curcio, Jenna Verrico, Sam

Maroon—the whole gang from the cafeteria. Three dozen kids with bicycles swarmed around Zack, Ms. DuBois, and Eddie.

"Hey, you're the new janitor!" said Benny. "Was that like a pretend Civil War pistol or a real one you were pointing at Zack?"

"I don't have a pistol. . . ."

"It's in your coat," said Rachel Curcio.

"Can we see the gun?" somebody else asked.

"My goodness," said Ms. DuBois, all sugar cookie-ish again, "whatever are all you children doing here at school on a Saturday?"

"We came to see what cool stuff Zack was getting into," said Benny. "Is this like a Civil War reenactment or something?"

Eddie laughed. "That's right." He pulled out his pistol. "And this here is a reproduction of a Colt Pietta, a Confederate army revolver from the 1860s. . . ."

"Coool!" The kids crowded closer.

"Zack and Mr., uh, Eddie, and I were working on a skit for history class!" said Ms. DuBois.

"Neat!"

"Can we touch the pistol?"

"Does it really work?"

And while Zack's three dozen friends swamped their two captors, Zack and Zipper backed away, ever so quietly, around the corner.

After that, they ran!

82

"Yes!"

Kurt Snertz saw Zack Jennings and his stupid little dog come running around the side of the school.

No teachers. No janitors. No friends.

They were dead meat.

Jennings yanked open a side door and darted into the building.

Snertz jumped up. He was going in after him.

He'd find a toilet and finally give Jennings that swirly.

But first he'd break a few of the geek's bones.

And drop-kick his dog up the hall!

Yes!

83

"Flip the flue!" Seth Donnelly said to his zombie.

"Yes, master."

His slave shoved the lever forward. A damper blocked one exhaust chimney and redirected the fumes to the second smokestack.

"Have him open the door!" shouted Joseph.

"Open the door to the smoke chamber!"

"Yes, master." The zombie shuffled over to the door. Opened it.

The corridor beyond was filling with a curling gray cloud.

"By jingo," cried Joseph. "It'll work! Keep the fire raging but divert the smoke back up to the main stack! Hurry! Tell him. He only listens to you!"

So Seth passed on the next set of commands.

The zombie strode back to the furnace. Shoved some levers.

"And have him leave the door open on this end! Best to air out the corridor so the grown-ups we send in don't suspect nothin'!"

"Joseph?"

"What, Seth?"

"I'm not your zombie. You can't keep bossing me around, telling me what to tell him."

"Who's gonna stop me, boy-o? You?"

Seth thought about that for a second. Joseph had been telling him what to do for 110 years and sometimes Seth just wanted to tell his big brother to stick a plug in his piehole.

But Joseph was all the family Seth had ever known. Their father had died before Seth was born; his mother while giving birth to him. He so longed to be set free from this place, this school, to be reunited up in heaven with the parents he'd never met.

But he wouldn't leave without Joe. Joe had looked out for him for 110 years. And Joe wouldn't leave until somebody paid for what Mr. Cooper had done.

"Leave the door open!" Seth barked at the zombie. "Let the room air out. We're gonna snag us a grown-up today!"

"We sure are, little brother. Why, I figure we might even trap us a pretty little teacher named Daphne DuBois, who just happens to be related to Mr. Patrick J. Cooper himself!"

"Hot diggity dog!" said Seth. "If we kill her, then we can surely rest in peace."

"Maybe, little brother," said Joseph. "Maybe."

And while the zombie fiddled with gauges and stoked the firebox, Joseph started whistling, then singing again.

Glory, glory, hallelujah
Teacher hit me with a ruler
Shot her in the butt with a rotten coconut
And she ain't gonna teach no more.

"Can that pistol blow stuff up?"

The boy named Benny kept asking Eddie the same silly question, over and over.

"Can it, like, shoot exploding fireballs and junk?"

Daphne DuBois kept smiling. Pretending to like these children, most of whom she knew from her nightmarish lunches in the cafeteria.

"All right, children," she said, putting on the sickly sweet voice she had used to fool them all into thinking she could tolerate their company. "Time for everybody to go home. Isn't that right, Zack? Tell your friends to go home. Zack?"

"He left," said Chuck Buckingham, the boy Daphne DuBois wished would just go have a heart attack and die already.

She started blinking. Couldn't control her twitching eyelids. "He left?"

"Yeah," said Benny. "Maybe he went to get a musket or something. Maybe a cannon. A cannon could blow up all sorts of stuff!"

"Eddie? Inside. Now! Children? Go home! Or I swear on my dead uncle's grave, I'll flunk every stinking one of you!"

The gaggle of giggly children instantly grew quiet.

The heartbroken clump of them just stood there.

The look on their faces?

Why, it made Ms. Daphne DuBois smile.

Zack and Zipper hurried down the staircase to the janitor's closet.

Zack shoved open the door and saw that Malik or Azalea or somebody had left the sliding shelving unit wide open.

He quickly grabbed a flashlight.

"Come on, Zip. Into the root cellar. I'll close the secret panel behind us."

But then Zack heard somebody thudding down the steps from the main building.

He wouldn't have time to close up the secret portal.

"Let's go!"

Zack and Zipper darted into the root cellar.

Zack whistled.

Zipper jumped up into his arms.

Zack sat down in front of the hole in the wall, worked his legs into the opening, and, snuggling Zipper, slid down the chute into the darkness.

Captain Pettimore had the girl's body stop when it reached the bottom of the thirty-nine steps.

This was his safe room.

He ignited the red and green kerosene lanterns dangling from the ceiling.

It felt good to do things again, simple things like striking a match, smelling the air, eating fried lard and eggs. He had done that at the girl's home this morning when he'd first entered her body at eight a.m. By eight a.m. tomorrow, any lingering trace of the soul once known as Azalea Torres would be gone.

For now, his soul shared this one body with her soul. But her soul was weak.

Actually, it was slumbering in a trance. A deep voodoo trance.

"Brother!"

Pettimore felt the heart in his new chest skip a beat. The ghost who'd just materialized had startled him.

"Hello, Mary." He had Azalea sneer at his long-dead sister. "My, you look pretty in your wedding dress. Did they actually allow you to wear white?"

"You must leave Azalea's body!"

He laughed. "Are you insane?"

"Leave her, Horace! I beg of you."

"Go away, Mary. You have done what you were born to do: You, through your offspring, have given me everlasting life. Now leave. Do not disgrace our family's good name yet again with your shameful deeds!"

"But . . ."

"By the way, I met your husband in a battlefield hospital down south. He died a coward, Mary, turning tail and running from the enemy. He brought indignity and shame to all those who bear his name. No wonder you two got along so well!"

Weeping, the ghost of Mary Jane Hopkins disappeared.

Laughing, Pettimore reached for the amulet he'd come to that room to find. It was suspended from a gold necklace, the one he had hung on that wall so long before. A tarnished silver disk embossed with a cryptic drawing:

He draped it around his neck and left the small room.

He walked about twenty paces, then, instead of continuing straight on to the old steamboat boiler, went up an intersecting passageway headed east.

Pettimore reached a T and turned right. Within minutes, he was at the base of the right-hand staircase. He was in the zombie pit.

McNulty was crouching in the darkness, waiting for him.

87

Kurt Snertz raced down the staircase to the basement, taking the steps two at a time.

He had seen Jennings and his dumb little dog run into a room to hide.

Kurt chuckled.

You can run but you cannot hide—not from me!

Swaggering, he sauntered up the hall. No need to run anymore. Jennings was trapped inside, believe it or not, the janitor's closet.

"Bad choice, lamebrain!" Kurt bellowed. "There's all sorts of stuff in there for me to smack you with. Broom handles. Mop handles. Toilet plungers!"

Snertz shoved open the door.

The closet was dark, so he couldn't see which corner scaredy-cat Jennings and his doofus dog were crouching in.

"Nice try, dipstick."

Kurt flicked up the light switch. He saw shelves lined with cleaning supplies. A floor-buffing machine. Cartons of paper hand towels.

But no Jennings. No dog.

Then he noticed an opening in the far wall, right behind

a set of shelves set at a screwy angle. It led to another room!

"Gee," Kurt said, chuckling, "I wonder where wacky Zacky could be hiding."

He made his way across the cramped closet, pushing boxes and coiled extension cords and cleaning crap out of his way.

"You are so dead, Jennings!"

He leapt through the opening.

Into another empty room. This one had a dirt floor and stacked stone walls. There were a couple of heavy metal-band posters taped up for decoration and a picture of that old Civil War geezer the school was named after. Shelves, too. Wooden ones. Lined with glass jars filled with moldy powders, rancid fruit, and pickled peppers.

"Gross," Kurt muttered.

Now he saw a hole in one of the walls.

He went over to it. Got down on his hands and knees and peered into some kind of chute, only wide and deep enough for one person to crawl through at a time.

There was a box full of junk on one of the shelves. Inside it, Kurt found a miniature flashlight. He twisted it on. Shone it into the hole.

"Jennings? Is this your rat hole, you lousy stinking rat? Don't make me come down there after you! Jennings?"

No answer.

"Okay. Now you are definitely gonna die!"

Furious, Kurt Snertz clenched the flashlight in his teeth and slid through the hole.

88

Zack thought he heard Kurt Snertz screaming something from way up at the entrance to the tunnel.

He didn't care. He needed to find Malik.

So Zipper and he kept walking forward. Zack swung his flashlight back and forth. He could see they were in some kind of very long mine shaft.

Zipper barked.

Ahead, a flashlight swirled around and a faint voice cried out, "Zipper?"

Malik!

"Malik? Is that you?"

"Zack?"

"Hang on! We're coming." Zack and Zipper started running straight for the quivering light.

"Don't be fooled by this body," Pettimore said to his slave. "It is I!"

"Yes, master."

Pettimore's neck felt stiff. This child's body didn't fit a soul of his size. No matter. In time, it would. The girl would grow. She'd eat all the richest foods in the world, because she would soon be the richest woman on earth!

Still, the captain missed a few of his ghostly abilities.

He could no longer flash into and out of portraits, see whatever he felt like seeing whenever he felt like seeing it. He couldn't keep his eyes on all those who would rob him of his treasure.

Again, no matter.

McNulty could do it for him.

"Slave, you are hereby granted permission to, for this day only, ignore the talisman at the top of this staircase. You may enter the long tunnel!"

The zombie drooled, sensing that it was feeding time.

"Stay within all the other boundaries I have marked for you, but slay anyone you see sliding down the chute from the root cellar! Slay them and gorge yourself on their brains!"

"Hurry!" said Malik. "I saw Azalea! Something's wrong with her . . . and . . . and . . . I really think there is some kind of zombie down here!"

Zack heard toenails clicking against wood.

Zipper started grumbling.

Zack felt hot breath on the back of his neck.

He swallowed hard.

Malik was trembling too much to raise his flashlight.

"Is somebody behind me, Malik?"

Malik nodded.

Zack heard another growl.

Deep. Rumbling. Full of phlegm.

It wasn't Zipper.

Slowly, very slowly, he turned around to see who or what was breathing down his neck.

91

"Hurry!" Daphne DuBois screamed at her brother as they rushed into the school building. "We need to find Zack. He's trying to steal the gold!"

"Look," said Eddie. "On the floor. Paw prints."

"That means Jennings and his dog came in here." Her tone brightened. "Follow the tracks! Foolish boy! He doesn't have much of a head start."

They headed up the hall, eyes glued to the paw prints dotting the floor.

"And, Edward? When we find young Zachary Jennings, will you kindly put one of your bullets in his brain?"

"Why, it would be my pleasure, Daphne. My absolute pleasure."

Zack had never seen anything so gruesomely hideous!

Pettimore's zombie stood nearly seven feet tall and had splotches of scraggly matted hair poking out around vein-riddled islands of scalp. His face was a skull wrapped in drum-tight skin. His fang-toothed smile cut across his cheekbones and crept up toward his ears.

But the worst parts were the bulging eyes. The dead and empty eyes popping out of their sockets.

Zack stepped backward.

"Stay back, Zip," he said without taking his eyes off the blank eyes staring at him.

Drool dribbled out between the thing's teeth. A drop splattered on the floor. Zack thought he heard it sizzle when it hit. Like battery acid.

The zombie was dressed in a tattered blue uniform—mostly shreds and threads. Zack could see his rippling leg muscles, the curling claws at the tips of gangly fingers and toes.

The jaw creaked open and Zack smelled sewer gas.

"You are trespassing," the thing said, his voice deep and rumbling.

"No . . . I just came . . . to get my friend. . . ."

"You came to rob my master's gold."

"No, like I said—"

The crouching thing hopped forward.

Zack leapt back.

Suddenly, from the far end of the tunnel, all the way back at the entrance, he heard a thud.

The zombie heard it, too. Hesitated.

"Jennings?"

Snertz.

The zombie perked up his ears.

"Where are you? I'm gonna kill you so bad. . . ."

One hundred yards away, a flashlight swirled around.

Phlegm rumbled in the zombie's massive chest. "Slay anyone I see sliding down the chute," the thing muttered. "Slay them and gorge on brains!"

In a blur of blue, the zombie started running up the tunnel, back toward the root cellar.

93

Kurt Snertz had to rethink how much he really wanted to kill Zack Jennings.

Because some kind of giant rat-dog with two glowing red eyeballs was galloping up the long, narrow tunnel toward him.

He looked at the hole in the wall he had just tumbled through.

There was something strange burned into the wood above the hole, a black tattoo he hadn't seen when he'd slid out:

Snertz had no idea what it meant.

He didn't have time to care.

He just knew he had to scramble back up to the hole as fast as he could, because the thing with the laser-pointer eyes was only fifty yards away!

94

"That's the zombie!" said Malik.

"Come on, we need to get out of here." Zack swung the flashlight back and forth. Twenty feet away on either side of the watch wall was the top of a staircase. "Zipper? Keep an eye up the tunnel while we figure which way to go."

Zipper hunkered down on all fours in his preferred prepare-to-pounce position.

"If that thing comes back . . ."

"I already figured it out," said Malik. "The pocket watches on the wall are another code!"

"Numbers for letters?"

Malik shook his head. "Semaphore flags!"

"Huh?"

"A system for sending messages by placing your arms, two flags, or, in this case, two clock hands in certain positions! They use it on ships all the time—to communicate with other ships."

"Stand *watch* like a sailor should and your prospects shall be very good!" said Zack, remembering the last line from the stone.

"Exactly."

"Malik, tell me you already translated this thing."

"Yes. It took me longer than anticipated, however. . . ."

"Which staircase?"

"The one on the left!"

Zack whistled; Zipper sprang up.

"Let's go!"

They raced down the steps, which were quite steep.

"Would you like to know how I figured it out?"

"Sure. Once we get away from that thing."

"I don't think the zombie is allowed to come down these steps."

"Really?"

"So the coded message would seem to say."

Breathing hard, after clomping down thirty-nine steps, they reached a landing.

"Okay," said Zack. "Tell me what you figured out."

"I propose," said Malik between gasps for oxygen, "that, whenever we're presented with a choice, we always head left."

"Really?"

Malik nodded. "Heading left will keep us zombie free."

Malik started making gestures, placing his left arm in the six o'clock position, his right at seven. "A." He raised his right arm to nine o'clock, so it was pointing straight out. "B." He nudged the right arm up and was about to say, "C," when Zack interrupted him.

"Um, maybe you could teach me the whole alphabet later?"

"Ah. Of course. The message on the wall says . . ."

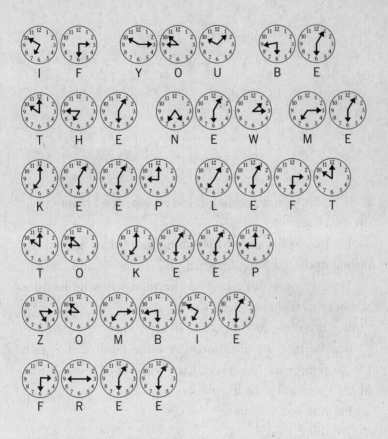

I F YOU BE
THE NEW ME
KEEP LEFT
TOKEEP
ZOMBIE
FREE

"The new me?" said Zack. "That could be Azalea!"

"Huh?"

"Captain Pettimore's soul somehow got inside Azalea's body!"

"Well, Zack, we need to get it out!"

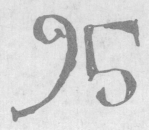

Kurt Snertz was clawing and clambering his way back up the chute.

He fought the slant by jamming his butt up against the ceiling and scrabbling forward on his elbows and knees.

He was only three feet up the tube when he heard a slobbery snarl below him.

But the thing did not climb in after him.

Maybe that weird tattoo was some kind of stop sign for giant gophers. Whatever. Kurt was out of the slide and in the room with the dirt floor.

He was going to live.

Jennings, too.

No way was Kurt Snertz sliding back down this coal chute to kill the wuss.

Not with a rabid gopher with laser-beam eyeballs growling up his butt.

Zipper, his paws poised on the first step, barked his warning bark up the staircase.

"He's back," said Zack.

"Is he coming down the stairs?" asked Malik.

Zack leaned over Zip. Listened hard. All he heard was some distant grumbling, like a caged lion eager to escape from the zoo.

"I think we're safe for now," said Zack. "We just need to find a way out of here."

"Well, we can't go out the way we came in."

Zack shone his flashlight around. "Let's keep moving forward. And, Malik?"

"Yes, Zack?"

"Thanks for figuring out the code."

"Well, I had a little time to kill. . . ."

Now they both heard the zombie growling angrily behind them.

But just as the pocket watches said, he didn't come down the left-hand tunnel after them.

97

Kurt Snertz ran out of the janitor's closet.

"You there!"

It was the new janitor, dressed like a golfer, and the blond history teacher, the one who was always busting Kurt's chops.

"Have you seen Zack Jennings?" the janitor asked.

"Maybe."

"Where is he?" asked the teacher.

"Why?"

"We have reason to believe," said the janitor, "that Mr. Jennings brought his dog to school today."

"Yeah. He did. Is he in trouble?"

"Big trouble," said the teacher. "Detention hall for life!"

"Awesome. He went in there." Kurt pointed toward the door he'd just come through. "There's like this other room connected to the first room and then there's this hole in the wall that leads to a—"

The teacher and the janitor didn't wait to hear the rest.

They shoved open the closet door and, from the sound of it, knocked over a bunch of boxes and plastic jugs as they made their way to the room with the dirt floor.

Man, they must want to punish Jennings bad!

98

Captain Pettimore finally piloted his new body to the boiler room and the smokestack chamber, his final defense against any intruders.

Now he saw an unknown man stoking the firebox.

"Who in blazes are you?" he had Azalea say for him.

The man turned around and Captain Pettimore could tell: He wasn't a man anymore. He had the unstaring, unseeing, unfocused eyes of a soulless zombie.

"Who turned you, boy? Who is your *bokor*? Your voodoo sorcerer?"

"He's ours, little girl!" two voices answered.

It was the Donnelly brothers. The blustering bully, Joseph, and Seth, the puny little clairvoyant whom the ghost of John Lee Cooper had once used to communicate with his kin, that foolish math teacher Patrick J. Cooper, one of the many Coopers to come north over the years to try to claim the captain's gold as their own.

In short, the Donnelly boys had aided and abetted his sworn enemies! He had Azalea sneer at them. "I am Horace P. Pettimore! How'd you two worthless souls master the voodoo to raise a zombie from the dead?"

"We didn't have to!" said the one called Joseph. "Yours bit the poor feller. Ain't that so, zombie?"

The zombie stood there drooling.

"Answer my brother," said the small one, Seth.

"Yes, master."

"Well done, Seth," Pettimore jeered through Azalea's lips. "You taught your zombie to speak. Bravo. You should know, then, that his fate is forever linked to the fate of the slave I call McNulty."

"Huh?" said the brutish boy, Joseph.

"If anything were to happen to my zombie, why, yours would simply become a man again, because you did not trap his soul in a jar, did you?"

"We didn't need to!"

That made Pettimore grin. "Perhaps. But I always found it wise to keep one's possessions tightly sealed and hidden away. Now, if you will excuse me . . ."

"Talking's not the only thing our zombie knows how to do, pal!" boasted Joseph. "Now that your spirit is walking around inside the body of a little girl, my brother can have his zombie rip you to shreds and eat out your brain."

"That's right," said Seth. "I can!"

Pettimore made the girl's lips curl even higher. "I'd like to see you try."

Seth hesitated. He clearly lacked the bloodlust to be a ruthless slave driver.

His brother, however, did not.

"Sic him, Seth! Do it now!"

"But she's a girl. . . ."

Pettimore laughed.

Perhaps that was a mistake.

Anger flared in the younger ghost's eyes. "Kill her!"

"Yes, master."

The zombie lurched forward.

Pettimore had Azalea calmly show the zombie the amulet dangling off her necklace:

It was the same symbol he used to corral his own zombie, to keep McNulty from straying where he did not want the beast to go.

"What is that chicken-scratching?" asked Joseph.

Pettimore had Azalea chuckle. "You two fresh fish have much to learn if you ever hope to become true voodoo masters. This is the veve of Baron Samedi, a loa of Haitian voodoo!"

"A what?"

"He is one of the mystères, the invisibles, the saints of

the voodoo religion! Baron Samedi is the loa of the dead! It is he who ferries souls to the underworld. No zombie dare anger him or attack a human under Samedi's protection!"

The zombie backed away.

"Now, boys, if you will excuse me. . . ."

Captain Pettimore had the girl walk over to the boiler and open the fourth firebox door on the furnace below, the door with flames painted on its glass window because it wasn't really a firebox at all. Pettimore had Azalea lift the latch and crawl inside. This part of the furnace was cold, an insulated cubbyhole with a bank safe for its floor, making it a trapdoor—if you knew the combination to the lock.

Captain Pettimore, of course, did. In fact, he was the one who, more than a century ago, had etched it into the steel walls.

CE-18, P-12, W-18

A simple back-and-forth numbers-letters code that translated to 35-R, 16-L, 23-R.

He opened the door in the floor and made Azalea climb down the ladder riveted to the wall.

"I'll be downstairs, lads. Collecting my treasure!"

Judy and George pulled into the driveway at the front of the school.

They had already driven around the cemetery loop road and hadn't seen Zack, the teacher, or anybody.

"Maybe they went back to a classroom," said George as they climbed out of the car with their pizza boxes.

"Would they let Zipper go into the school?"

"Maybe. . . ." Then George stuck a thumb and forefinger into his mouth and let out a piercing whistle, the kind that could stop taxicabs in Times Square.

Judy almost dropped her pizza.

"He usually comes when I whistle like that," George explained.

Judy's ears were ringing.

She'd be surprised if the whistle didn't wake the dead people back in the cemetery!

100

Zack, Zipper, and Malik were sitting in a small room, staring at the wild inscription on the wall:

"Any idea what it is?" Zack asked.

"Some kind of voodoo symbol," said Malik. "Probably painted with chicken blood."

"Gross. We need to find where Pettimore stored his soul jars."

"You mean there's another root cellar?"

"Sort of. See, when the *bokor* steals a dead person's soul, he captures the *ti bonanj,* the part of our spirit that holds whatever it is that makes you and me unique and different from everybody else. . . ."

"Did you look this up on Google?"

"Last night. A friend gave me a heads-up on what we might be facing."

"Who? Benny?"

"That's not important. What's important is—"

Suddenly, Zipper's ears perked up.

"He hears something!" said Malik. "The zombie?"

"No. His tail's wagging. He's not afraid. He's happy."

Zipper looked up at Zack and gave him a series of short barks.

"What's he trying to say?" asked Malik.

"I don't know. It's not one of his standard barks."

And then Zipper took off!

"Where's he going?" asked Malik.

"Back the way we came . . ."

"What about the zombie?"

"I don't think they like dog brains. Just humans'."

Malik sighed. "I sort of wish I were a dog."

"Come on. Let's go see what's up ahead."

101

"This is it," said Daphne DuBois, staring at the scorched hole in the wall. "The entrance to the treasure tunnel."

"There's a stone on the ground," said Eddie. "See it? What do all those strange carvings mean?"

"That's the Masons' code," said Daphne, pulling out her spiral notebook, the one filled with all sorts of information related to the treasure quest. She found the page dealing with the code and quickly translated the stone's message.

"It mentions a zombie," she said.

Eddie laughed. "The old carpetbagger is bluffing! Colonel Cooper told Zack Jennings in no uncertain terms, 'There are no more booby traps in the tunnels, no more guards.'"

"Yes. The boy would never have been brave enough to crawl into that hole if he thought there might be a zombie at the other end waiting for him!"

"I'll go in first," said Eddie. "Grab a couple of those candles off the shelf."

She did. Eddie lit them.

Daphne smiled. "Now let's go get our gold!"

102

Daphne watched Eddie slide down the chute.

When he hit the ground with a soft thump, Daphne crawled into the hole. She was all set to slide down to join her brother when she heard him scream.

"Leave me be!"

Next Daphne heard an angry roar and thrashing and Eddie shrieking.

"No! Stop!"

More howls and bellowing. The shredding of cloth. Snarls and rips and the crunching of bone and sloppy wet feeding sounds.

She blew out her candle.

Bracing her hands against the ceiling, her feet against the floor, she crept down the sharply inclined tube. She moved very slowly, very cautiously, the whole time serenaded by the sounds of someone greedily stuffing his face with food.

"Mmmm . . . good . . . brains . . ."

She reached the bottom. Crawled feetfirst into some kind of darkened cave.

Eddie's black wax candle lay on the floor, still sputtering, still casting a faint glow—enough light for Daphne to see the most horrific thing she had ever seen in her life.

A lanky beast in a frayed Yankee soldier uniform scooping curdled gray matter out of her brother's cracked-open skull and slurping it into his mouth.

103

Zack and Malik kept moving forward.

The tunnels were chilly, dark, and quiet. The narrow passageways turned back on themselves at abrupt angles. Whenever the path split, they headed left—just like the pocket watches had told them to.

"Thanks again, Zack," Malik whispered.

"For what?"

"Being my friend. Coming down to find me."

"No problem."

"You think that thing killed Kurt Snertz?"

"I hope not."

They walked some more.

"If we actually find the gold," said Malik, "I'll split it with you!"

"That's okay. You keep it. I just want to go home and play with Zip in the backyard!"

They kept walking.

Downhill.

Working their way deeper into the labyrinth.

The zombie's lair.

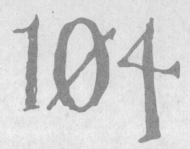

The beast was licking his spindly fingers.

It pained Daphne DuBois to see her brother this way. Torn asunder. His pants and legs lying in a heap to the left. His jacket and torso to the right.

His head hollowed out like a Halloween pumpkin.

But she had to press on.

For Edward Cooper DuBois.

For Patrick J. Cooper and John Lee Cooper! For every son of the Confederacy humiliated by the Union aggressors when the noble cause ran out of money because the scoundrel Horace P. Pettimore ran off with the shipment of English gold!

She saw Eddie's revolver lying on the ground near the gnawed remains of his right arm.

The beast seemed momentarily satiated. Gorging on her brother's meaty brain appeared to have made him drowsy.

She saw the creature's bulging eyes disappear beneath their reptilian lids.

Very quietly, she reached down and took the pistol.

Then, turning away from the beast, she started trotting

quietly down a long, straight tunnel. After about fifty feet, she lit her own candle. Held it out in front of her.

Ahead she saw a wall full of pocket watches.

The straightaway ended. She had a choice. A staircase twenty feet to her right. A staircase twenty feet to her left.

She could not decide which way to go.

She needed help. A spirit guide!

"Colonel Cooper?" she whispered. "Can you hear me?"

There came no ghostly reply. Frustrated, she stomped her feet. "Grandfather!" she whined. "Tell me which way I should go!"

One hundred yards behind her, she heard the beastly thing bay. Heard him rumble like a dragon.

She probably shouldn't have raised her voice like that.

A loud roar shook the rafters.

Daphne DuBois ran as fast as she could down the staircase on the left.

105

Judy saw Zipper tear out the front door of the school.

"George! It's Zip!"

"Hey, boy." George knelt down.

The dog practically trampolined off the asphalt and into his arms.

And then he wouldn't stop barking.

"Where's Zack?" George asked.

Zipper barked more loudly.

"Is he in trouble?" asked Judy.

He gave a bark that sounded an awful lot like "Yes!" Followed by a series that sounded like "Hurry! Follow me!"

"Take us to him, Zip!"

Zipper flew back into the school.

Judy and George flew after him.

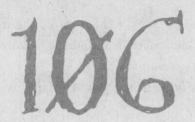

106

A *slow-moving* car pulled into the driveway at the front of the school.

A young African American girl—about eight years old with caramel-colored skin, her hair piled up under a bright yellow head scarf, her cheeks freckled with dots of black paint—stepped out. She was carrying a small burlap sack.

"Wait for me here, Auntie," she said. "I shan't be long."

The little girl marched toward the school, quietly singing a snatch of her favorite song.

> *My grandma see your grandpa sitting by the fire*
> *My grandpa say to your grandma, gonna fix your*
>   *chicken wire.*
> *Talkin' 'bout, hey now, hey now. Iko, iko on day.*

A sly smile slid across her lips.

"*Joc-a-mo-fee-no-ah-nah-nay,*" she mumbled. "*Joc-a-mo-fee-nah-nay.*"

It was a ritual chant used in New Orleans by marchers

in Mardi Gras parades, a chant so old the words were no longer clear, but loosely translated, "Jockomo feena nay" meant, "Don't mess with us."

This little girl from New Orleans was nobody to mess with.

107

The ghost of Horace Pettimore stared through Azalea Torres's eyes at the mountain of shimmering gold bars stacked floor to ceiling in his hidden vault.

He propelled the girl's body closer to the pile. Each bar weighed 12.4 kilograms. About 27 pounds. There were hundreds of them.

He had the girl grab a bar, hoist it off the pile, and load it into her backpack.

"Ummpfff . . ."

It strained her weak arms.

She would never be able to carry this treasure lode up to the surface and exchange it for money.

"McNulty!" he had her shout. "McNulty! Come here! I need you! I need you now!"

108

Daphne DuBois was catching her breath in a small chamber with a strange drawing on the wall when she heard something even stranger: Azalea Torres shouting for somebody named McNulty.

"Come here! I need you! I need you now!"

Then she heard what sounded like horse hooves thundering down the corridor at the top of the stairs.

The zombie.

But he didn't come down the left side! He must have gone right!

The slobbering beast who had devoured her brother was no longer pursuing her.

She forged on.

"I do this for all the Coopers who came this way before me," she vowed under her breath.

And Eddie. Her little brother.

He would not die in vain!

109

McNulty scampered down the steep staircase.

When he reached his killing pit, he took the tunnel to his left.

Followed it to where it would enter the steamship boiler room.

But the master was not in that room.

He was down below.

In the gold vault.

McNulty was too tall to fit inside the furnace cubbyhole and take the ladder down to the treasure chamber. He would need to find a different way to reach his master.

He followed the tunnel into the darkness.

His nostrils flared as he attempted to pick up the master's scent.

It was no good. He kept running. Deeper. Downhill. Dark.

"McNulty!"

His master's voice!

Behind an earthen wall.

It did not matter.

McNulty was strong. He ripped through the dirt and the rock and the mortar. The wall crumbled. Now he was in a tiny sealed room. Many glass jars lined the shelves.

"McNulty!"

The master was close. The other side of another wall. McNulty needed to break through. The next wall was thick. A vault wall. Cinder blocks. Bricks.

"McNulty!"

He saw a steel support pillar in the center of the room. Grunting, he hoisted it up out of the ground, taking out a chunk of the ceiling, sending dirt and debris showering all around him.

"McNulty!"

"Coming, master!"

He used the steel girder like a battering ram and slammed and slammed and slammed it against the treasure vault wall until the cement blocks broke free.

Through the hole in the wall, he saw his master, who was now a girl, standing in a chamber, surrounded by shimmering gold bricks.

"There you are, McNulty. What in blazes took you so long?"

110

Judy and George followed Zipper to the janitor's closet and the root cellar and the slide to the tunnel.

"I've never been down here before," said George as he stood up and dusted off the seat of his pants.

"Me neither," said Judy.

"This mine shaft cuts clear across the soccer field! No wonder a strip of snow always . . ."

"Always what?"

George had made the mistake of looking to his right.

Zipper whimpered.

"There's . . . a body . . . body parts . . . strewn all over. . . . I think I'm gonna be sick."

And he was.

111

Zack and Malik rounded a bend and came into a room where the air smelled like a roaring fireplace at Christmastime.

They heard a chugging engine, its piston arm rocketing back and forth, steam hissing out its sides.

And then they saw the back of a man feeding firewood into a red-hot furnace.

"I think that's the old janitor," whispered Malik. "I think his name is Wade."

"Wade?" Zack called out.

The man kept loading lumber into the firebox.

"Hey, is that the boiler for the school?" Zack asked. Then he tried to make a joke. "Boy, talk about your long commute . . ."

Now the man turned around. He wasn't laughing.

He wasn't all there, either.

His eyes were dull and glazed over. He moved with a staggered gait. The guy had to be the second zombie Mr. Willoughby had warned him about!

That was when the Donnelly brothers materialized.

"Well, hey there, sport," said Joseph. "Long time no see. We don't need to bum a match off you no more. Our zombie brought his own."

The beast lurched forward a step.

"Stop!" said Seth.

The zombie froze.

"That's right," said Joseph. "You don't get to eat your supper until we say so!"

"Leave these two boys alone," added Seth.

"Yes, master." The janitor zombie lowered his head and retreated two steps.

Zack felt Malik tugging at his sleeve.

"Zack?"

"Yeah?"

"What are you staring at?"

"The Donnelly brothers."

"They're dead."

"Yeah. They know."

Joseph Donnelly strode across the room. "Who's your pal here, Zack?"

"Malik. I don't think he can see ghosts."

"Are they talking to you?" asked Malik.

"He can't hear you, either."

"You two come all the way down here looking for the treasure?" asked Joseph.

"Yes," said Zack.

"What'd the dead boy ask you?" said Malik.

"He asked if we came for the gold."

"We did! My mother needs some medicine real bad and . . ."

"Boo-hoo-hoo," scoffed Joseph. "Malik's trying to help his mommy. Well, guess what? We don't have no mother—and no father, neither."

Zack pointed toward a propped-open door at the far end of the room. "What's through that door?"

"Nothing."

"Then why is there a door on the other side?"

"Because."

"Aw, cut it out, Joseph," said Seth. "Malik is trying to help his mom."

"Oh, you think because you have a zombie to boss around, you can boss me around, too?"

"No, I'm just saying we should let these two be. It's the teacher we're after!"

"Ms. DuBois?" said Zack.

That got both the brothers' attention.

"She's probably right behind us."

"Glory, glory, hallelujah!" said Joseph, who now seemed anxious for Zack and Malik to be gone. "Boys, you just earned yourself a free pass. Proceed through that door. Walk through the little chamber and out the door at the other end. Go through it but—and this is the most important part—make sure you lock it. Lower the iron bar on the other side."

"Why?" asked Zack.

"If you don't, Seth here will sic his zombie on you."

"That's right. I will," Seth said with a wink. He was

just pretending to be tough to keep his brother happy, but Zack could tell that the younger ghost was doing them a favor.

"Okay, we'll lower the bar," said Zack.

"If you don't do like we told you, we'll know," said Joseph. "We can see through walls, boy-o. Heck, we can walk through 'em, too."

"Any idea what's on the other side of the second door?" Zack asked.

"Another tunnel," said Seth. "But if you're clever, it'll take you down to the captain's gold."

"What'd they say?" asked Malik.

"We walk through that chamber, go out the door at the other end, lock the door behind us, and we're on our way to the gold!"

"Yes!" said Malik.

"Hey, Zack?" said Seth. "If you find that gold, will you really give it to your friend's mom?"

"That's the plan."

"Then hurry! The teacher will be here soon!"

"Hold on," said Zack. "We're also looking for another friend. A girl named Azalea. Black hair. Black fingernails. Black eye makeup and lipstick. Did she come down this way?"

"Nope," said Joseph. "We sure didn't see no girl. Heck, there hasn't been a *girl* down here in years."

Seth nodded in agreement.

But then he winked again.

112

Zack and Malik hurried through the open door and entered a room about the size of a walk-in closet.

The walls were streaked with black, the air tinged with the scent of wood smoke.

Zack looked up. Saw the fluted end of a smokestack.

"There's the other door!" said Malik, pointing ahead. "Hurry!"

They went out the door.

"Close it!" said Malik.

They shoved it shut.

"Lower the latch."

Zack lowered the heavy iron bar.

"Good," said Malik. "Now the janitor zombie and Ms. DuBois can't come after us!"

Zack just hoped Malik was right.

113

George draped his jacket over as much of the corpse as he could.

Zipper slumped to the ground, his tail tucked between his legs.

"This is horrible. What's going on down here?"

"Something unbelievably bad," said Judy, almost as if she were talking to herself. "Why didn't Zack tell me?"

"*You?* Why didn't he tell me?"

"Because you wouldn't have believed him."

"What?"

"This was done by some sort of supernatural beast. A werewolf or a ghoul or a . . ."

"Or a zombie."

"What? You don't believe in zombies or ghouls or ghosts. Right?"

"Sure he does," said a kindly voice in the darkness.

Judy whipped her flashlight around. Its beam reflected off a white crossing-guard sash.

"Scary Arie?" said George.

"Hiya, George."

"Honey?" said Judy.

"Judy, uh, meet Arie Sibirski. In 1949, he died saving a kid in a crosswalk."

"Darn turnip truck," groused Arie.

"He's a ghost?" said Judy.

"Yeah."

"And you can see him?"

"You see him, too, right?" George asked Judy.

"Yeah. So that's where Zack gets it. . . ."

"Zack sees ghosts? He never told me."

"Did you ever tell anybody?"

"Are you kidding? They would've thought I was . . ." He paused for a second. "Oh. Yeah."

"Zack your son?" asked Arie.

"Yes."

"He and a friend named Malik went down to the end of the tunnel and took the staircase on the left."

"Thanks! Come on, Judy."

Arie flipped up a handheld stop sign. "Sorry. It's not safe down there."

"That's why we have to find Zack!"

"No, I mean it's not safe for you two."

"Sorry, Arie." George grabbed Judy by the hand. "Our son needs us. We're breaking the stupid rules!"

114

The eight-year-old girl in the yellow head scarf marched into the school, went left, toward the cafeteria, headed down a flight of steps, and entered the janitor's closet.

She had never been in the building before.

In fact, she had never journeyed beyond the borders of Louisiana.

But she knew exactly where she was going.

"*Joc-a-mo-fee-no-ah-nah-nay,*" she mumbled. "*Joc-a-mo-fee-nah-nay.*"

115

George Jennings could not believe he was seeing ghosts again.

It had been nearly twenty-two years since he had lost "the gift." And he hadn't missed it. Never told anybody he'd ever had it, either. Not his dad. Not his first wife. Not Zack. Not Judy.

"I haven't seen Arie since I was thirteen," he said out loud as he and Judy followed Zipper down a long tunnel. "He helped me win my first case."

"How?" Judy asked.

"Mr. Crumpler, the assistant principal, accused my friend Stinky Seiden of stealing chocolate milk from the cafeteria. Arie led me to evidence showing that one of Mr. Crumpler's favorites, the football captain, was the one stealing the milk, not Stinky. I stood up for my friend. He was exonerated. Mr. Crumpler was publicly humiliated."

"No wonder he doesn't like Zack."

"Wow. My son sees ghosts. You do, too?"

Judy shrugged. "I see talking cats, too. . . ."

They reached a wall full of pocket watches and the two staircases. They followed Zipper down the steps to the left and entered a maze.

Zipper sniffed the air. Barked.

"He's picking up Zack's scent!" said Judy. "Run, Zip, run!"

116

Zipper's snout had a laser lock on his boy.

Zack's special odor. Better than bacon.

Left, left, left.

Dogs were much better at mazes than humans were.

Especially if their special someone had already gone through it before them!

117

Breathing hard, George and Judy raced after Zipper, who was zooming through the maze.

George sniffed the air. "Do you smell that?"

"Yeah. Smoke."

"Oh, boy. I hope Zack didn't start another fire."

118

"Careful!" said Zack.

He and Malik were in another tunnel, about ten feet away from the back door to the small chamber.

The floor seemed to shimmy and quiver.

There was a huge sinkhole dead ahead. A thick cloud of dust hovered over it.

Cautiously, Zack crept to the lip of the crater, knelt down, and shone his flashlight into the pit. To his surprise, there was another chamber under the tunnel they were in.

"There's a lower level!" he whispered to Malik.

Zack swung his beam around the hazy room below. Its floor was littered with chunks of rocky debris. The walls were lined with wooden shelves. Now the flashlight glinted off glass. Zack could vaguely make out several rows of dusty jars. Maybe it was another root cellar.

"We need to be down there!" Zack whispered to Malik.

Then, as quietly as they could, the two boys jumped into the dark room below.

119

Judy, George, and Zipper raced around a corner and entered what looked and felt like a furnace room.

They saw a drooling man holding a revolver on Zack's teacher, Ms. DuBois.

"Where's my son?" George shouted.

"What are you two doing down here?" the teacher hissed.

"We're looking for Zack!" said Judy.

"So am I," the teacher said sweetly, batting her eyes. "But this brute took my pistol. Be a dear, Mr. Jennings, and help me retrieve it."

"Your *pistol?*" said George, who wasn't going anywhere near the drooling man, who looked like he was dead, even though he was standing up and holding a gun.

"Don't listen to her," said the younger of two ghosts who suddenly materialized in front of the furnace.

"You're Seth Donnelly, right?" said Judy very tenderly.

The boy smiled. "Yes, ma'am. I sure am."

"Knock it off, little brother. She's a grown-up."

"She's a mom."

"So? Moms are grown-ups, too." Joseph turned to Judy. Puffed up his chest. "Do we know you, lady?"

"No."

"Then how do you know us?"

"I went to the library."

"Who the devil are you talking to?" demanded Ms. DuBois.

Judy and George pointed. "The two boys," said Judy. "The Donnelly brothers."

"You can see ghosts? Of course! Zack gets his special powers from you two! His parents! What's on the other side of that door? The one in the small chamber there."

"How should I know?"

"Ask your dead friends!"

George moved closer to the two ghost boys. "Where's Zack?"

"He's safe," said Seth.

"Did he and Malik go through that door?"

"Yep," said Joseph. "They sure did. Then they jumped down a rabbit hole. You should've seen 'em. Landed on their keisters! Guess they want that gold bad, huh?"

"I don't care about the stupid gold!" said George, wildly flapping his arm toward the open door to the small chamber. "But if that's where Zack and Malik went to find it . . ."

Ms. DuBois's eyebrows shot up when she heard that.

"Get out of my way!" She shoved George aside, ran for the door, jumped into the chamber, and slammed the door tight behind her.

"Lock it!" Joseph shouted to the drooling man at the furnace, who didn't budge. "Seth? Tell your slave to lock her in!"

The man looked to the young boy, who nodded sadly.

"Yes, master."

Joseph cackled with laughter.

The man lumbered over to the door and dropped a heavy steel brace into a bracket.

"Pump in the smoke!" shouted Joseph, and once again Seth nodded.

"Yes, master."

The zombie returned to the furnace and shoved a huge lever forward.

"What are you doing?" shouted George.

"What that no-good, two-faced teacher done to us!" Joseph shouted back.

And then one Donnelly brother sobbed while the other one just laughed and laughed and laughed.

120

The room they had dropped into had six solid walls, no doorway.

But that hadn't stopped someone from entering it: There were huge holes bashed through two of the thick stone walls. Flickering light fluttered through the far opening, from which Zack heard clinking and someone who sounded like Azalea on a really bad day barking orders: "More! Load the backpack!"

Zack raised a finger to his lips. Malik nodded.

In the dim light, Zack could see a steel support beam lying in a pile of rubble. Probably why the ceiling, which had been Zack and Malik's floor, had opened up into a sinkhole.

Why was this room sealed off from all the others? Zack wondered.

"Check out the jars," whispered Malik. "On the shelves and on the floor. Only one has a lid."

"There's something written on the sides," Zack whispered back. "See the labels?"

"Yeah."

"They look like names."

"What's the one with the lid say?" asked Malik.

Zack took it off the shelf. The glass felt warm, and something glimmered inside. "McNulty."

They heard a thud and clank of something heavy falling to the floor. Carrying the jar, Zack crept closer to the hole in the far wall.

"You weakling!" shouted the voice that sounded like Azalea's. "Surely you can carry more than that! Pile those bars on top of each other!"

Zack gripped the edge of a broken cinder block and peeked into the adjoining chamber—a room filled with shimmering bars of gold stacked ten feet tall, maybe ten feet deep.

"Faster, McNulty! I want to haul two dozen bars out of here before midnight tonight!"

"Yes, master."

Azalea wasn't alone.

The zombie was with her. And apparently, his name was McNulty.

Just like the name on the jar.

121

Judy heard Ms. DuBois's fists pounding against the door.

"You'll kill her!"

Joseph Donnelly's grin grew wider. "That's the plan, ma'am!"

"And then we can go home, right, Joe?" Seth pleaded.

"Maybe, little brother. Maybe."

George bolted for the door, got his hands on the lock bar, started prying it up.

"Stop him!" shouted Seth. "I want to leave this place!"

The zombie leapt across the room and, with super-human strength, grabbed hold of George and yanked him away from the door.

"I promised Joe he could have the teacher! She's evil!"

"But killing is wrong!" said Judy, moving closer to Seth.

Too close.

The zombie, holding George off the ground with one hand, strode across the room and grabbed Judy with the other.

"Protect master!"

When Zipper nipped at his ankles, the thing kicked the dog sideways, sending him skittering across the floor into the concrete slab holding up the broiling furnace.

Zipper yelped.

122

Zack heard his dog yelp.

And then what sounded like his father shouting: "Where's my son?"

And Judy: "Put me down!"

His parents were in trouble—and somewhere close.

He peered into the gold chamber. Saw a ladder bolted to the wall. It had to go back up to the furnace room. And since Malik and he couldn't climb up the way they'd come down . . .

"I'm going in," he whispered to Malik.

"Are you crazy? There's a zombie in there with Azalea, who isn't really Azalea right now!"

"Don't worry. I have his soul!"

"What?"

Zack didn't answer. He climbed through the hole and into the room filled with gold.

123

"You!" Captain Pettimore snarled through Azalea. "You're the boy I thought would be the one!"

Zack's eyebrows arched up. He had no idea what the man inside his friend was blabbing about.

"Kill him, McNulty!"

The giant flew across the room.

Zack held up the glass jar.

"Remember this?" he said to the beast.

The zombie froze.

"It's your soul. It's who you really are, not who Pettimore tells you to be!"

Zack smashed the jar down hard against the stone floor.

The zombie's eyes opened wide.

Golden light, like a squadron of fireflies, zoomed up from the shattered glass and smacked the zombie square in the chest. He recoiled in shock. Surprise and joy and sunshine filled his face as he drew in one long breath.

"My name is Cyrus McNulty," he said slowly. "I come from Indiana."

"That's right," said Zack. "Welcome home."

As McNulty smiled, his face seemed to bake—to dry out like mud in the sun. In an instant, it was crackled and brittle. In another, it crumpled into dust like it should have done back in 1864. The dead man's empty rags drifted to the floor.

McNulty was gone.

"Come on!" Zack called to Malik as he ran to the ladder. "The other one's upstairs and he doesn't have a soul jar!"

Malik raced across the room and followed Zack up the rungs.

Azalea tried to chase after the two boys.

But she had loaded her backpack down with too much gold and could barely move!

124

The zombie holding Judy and George let go of them and sank to the floor.

Then he started quivering.

"Dude," he mumbled.

It sounded like he was dreaming.

125

When Zack reached the top of the ladder, he was inside some kind of box.

Malik was two rungs behind him.

"You killed her!" he heard Judy cry.

"That's right." Joseph Donnelly's voice. "Just like her no-account relative Patrick J. Cooper killed us!"

"The hero teacher?"

"He weren't no hero, lady! He put a bullet in our brains and set that fire. Tried to make it look like we were the ones who done it! He got his, though. The door to his classroom locked behind him. He couldn't escape, neither. Died with us, went straight to hell. Me and Joe stuck around 'cause some new grown-up had to pay for what that greedy gold-grubbing teacher done to us!"

Zack finally realized why Davy and Mr. Willoughby wouldn't let him talk to any adults about what was going on underneath the school. They'd end up dead. The Donnellys would kill them.

"We're done now." The voice of Seth.

"No, we're not! We're gonna kill these two, too!"

"No, we are not!"

"Yes, we are!"

"Malik?" Zack said in a quick whisper. "Stay in here. Keep your eye on Azalea."

"Okay."

Zack sprang out of the box, tumbled to the ground.

The first thing he saw was Zipper lying on his side. Whimpering.

Zack scrambled to his feet. Realized he had just crawled out of the furnace underneath the boiler in the same room where he and Malik had been before they went through the back door to the small room.

"Zack!" shouted Judy and his father.

"Where's the zombie?"

Judy pointed to a heap on the floor. "Out cold."

"We were told he'd lose his zombification," said Seth, "if the one who bit him found his soul. Did you do that for Mr. McNulty, Zack?"

"Yeah, Seth. I did." He bent down to pet Zip, who thumped his tail. "Who hurt my dog?"

"The zombie," said Joseph. "It wasn't us."

Zack was fuming. "But you guys told him to do it!"

"Not really," said Joseph. "Besides, the zombie only listens to Seth, not me. So if you're gonna blame anybody—"

And that was when Davy appeared. "All right," he said to the Donnelly brothers. "You boys got your revenge. Ain't no reason to haunt here no more. Time to move on."

"Thank you!" said Seth.

"B-b-but . . . ," stammered Joseph.

"Vamoose, Joseph. Daniel Boone hisself wants a word with you. Davy Crockett, too!"

The Donnelly brothers disappeared.

Davy moved closer to Zack.

"I gotta go, pardner. Need to escort the Donnelly boys up to their tribunal. They'll go easy on Seth."

"What about Joseph?"

"Can't rightly say. Folks upstairs will see that justice gets done."

Zack nodded.

"You done good, Zack. Real good. We didn't think nobody could go up against Horace P. Pettimore and his zombies. But, dang—you sure did!"

"I finally figured out why you wouldn't let me tell any adults about what was going on. Guess the rules are there for a reason."

"Sometimes," Davy said with a wink. "Sometimes."

And then he vanished.

Zack's dad raised a hand. "Um, isn't that the boy who used to . . ."

Judy laughed. "Yes, honey."

"So he was a ghost, even then?"

"Yep," said Zack. "He sure was."

The fake furnace door swung open.

"Zack?" said Malik.

And then Azalea shoved him out of her way and crawled into the room.

126

"Thought you could come down here and steal my gold, did you?" said Azalea as she stumbled around the furnace chamber, her heavy backpack tilting her backward, throwing her off balance.

"Azalea?" said Zack's dad.

"She's not really herself right now," said Zack. "She's possessed by the spirit of Horace P. Pettimore."

"*The* Horace P. Pettimore?"

"Yeah. His soul snuck inside Azalea so he could live again and retrieve his gold."

"It's downstairs," added Malik. "Tons of it."

"So," said Judy, "do we need to find an exorcist or something?"

"Cut the chin music, you gallinippers!" grumbled Azalea. "I'm not pulling up stakes without my gold!"

"I don't know what to do!" said Zack.

A young girl stepped into the room.

"Don't worry, brother. I do."

She looked like she was maybe eight. She wore a yellow head scarf and had strange black markings painted on her caramel-colored cheeks.

"Greetings, Cap'n Pettimore. We meet again, no?"

Azalea stumbled backward in horror. "No! You?"

"Yes, Cap'n. I remember the night you killed me. You thought you were oh so clever. Well, Cap'n, the teacher, she always know more than the pupil, no?"

The girl pulled a glass jar out of a burlap sack.

"Queen LaSheena?" Azalea sputtered out the words.

"Yes." The little girl slowly twisted the lid on her jar and opened it. "My spy dog see your spy dog, no? For many years, I watch you and wait for you to make this mistake. I know all about the charm you bury in front of your mansion to lure your descendant to this place. I know everything. And so I wait for you to be foolish and greedy and put your soul inside a human body, where I can so easily snatch it."

"But . . . I have gold. . . ."

"I have more. . . ."

"Tell me what you want! I'll give it to you!"

"I only want the one thing, Cap'n."

"What?"

"Your immortal soul!"

She quickly chanted words Zack had never heard before. They were angry, short, and sharp.

Then she slammed the lid on top of the jar and tightened it.

Azalea slumped to the floor.

"Is my friend your zombie now?" Zack asked.

The little girl shook her head. "No. She will be fine.

Tomorrow, she will not remember a thing. It will all be a bad dream. But Cap'n Pettimore? He is now a zombie of the soul. He belong to me for all eternity."

She held up the jar. Stared at the amber glow flickering inside.

"*Joc-a-mo-fee-no-ah-nah-nay,*" she mumbled. "Don't mess with me, Cap'n!"

127

That night, all sorts of people were clustered in the main entrance to the school, right below the portrait of Horace P. Pettimore.

First came the police and paramedics, who took Azalea and the janitor Wade to the hospital, Ms. DuBois and her brother to the morgue. The first detectives on the scene had a theory that the brother and sister had died in a domestic dispute: They both wanted the gold, but they didn't want to share it. So Ms. DuBois hired an attack dog, while her brother relit Captain Pettimore's boiler and tricked his sister into going into the smoky chamber, where she suffocated when the door locked behind her.

Zack's dad, Judy, Malik, and Zack did not feel compelled to disagree with the detectives.

While the police issued an all-points bulletin for a "giant attack dog," Judy rushed Zipper to the closest animal hospital just to make sure that the zombie kick to his ribs hadn't broken any bones.

Zack's dad used his cell phone to call Malik's father, who came racing over to the school. While they waited for the police to finish their work and haul the gold up from the basement, Zack's dad and Mr. Sherman talked about how proud they both were of their brave sons. After a while, Mr. Sherman told Zack's dad all about how sick Malik's mom was and how they didn't have health insurance right then.

That was when the assistant principal, Carl D. Crumpler, stormed into the building.

"Jennings?" he screamed at Zack and his dad, who were standing in a corner with Malik and Mr. Sherman. "What goes on here?"

Zack's dad put his arm around Malik's shoulders.

"Well, Mr. Crumpler, my client, Malik Sherman—"

"Your client?"

"That's right. He needs someone to help him manage his money."

"What?"

"Mr. Sherman and Mr. Wade Muggins, a janitor here at the school, a man of great initiative, uncovered a coded stone left in the old root cellar by Horace P. Pettimore."

"What root cellar?" Mr. Crumpler had never looked more flustered.

"Showing great courage and determination, the two of them found what has eluded so many for so long: Captain Pettimore's stolen Confederate gold."

"Stolen?"

"Well, I'm sure the statute of limitations has expired, and the aggrieved party, the Confederate States of America, no longer exists. Therefore, it will be the recommendation of the Pettimore Trust that some reward money be given to both Mr. Sherman and Mr. Muggins. . . ."

"The *boy* and the *janitor*?"

"That's right. We also feel a donation should be made to the Fund for Extraordinary Young Girls in New Orleans."

"What?"

"Oh, it was one of Captain Pettimore's favorite charities. The bulk of the treasure will, of course, be transferred to the Pettimore Trust so we might continue doing the good works we know the captain would want us to do."

Zack nearly burst out laughing. That was the biggest fib of the night.

"I don't like this, Jennings. Something smells funny."

"Perhaps that's sour milk you're smelling, sir. Sour *chocolate* milk?"

That shut Crumpler up.

"Now, let's go help them inventory the gold," said Zack's dad, leading the way to the cafeteria, where the bars were slowly being transferred from the treasure tunnels.

While the adults streamed out of the main building, Zack turned to Malik.

"Congratulations," he said.

"Wow! They're really gonna give me a reward so I can help my mom?"

"Sure sounds like it."

"Thanks, Zack!"

"Hey, you earned it!"

"So," Malik whispered, "can you really see ghosts?"

"Yeah. But don't tell anybody, okay? My dad didn't even know until today."

They knocked knuckles on it.

"Hey, are there any ghosts in here now?"

Zack looked around the room. Didn't see anybody.

Except . . . yes . . . stepping through the wall underneath the Pettimore portrait.

"Just one."

"Really? Who is it?"

"A young guy. He used to fly with the Tuskegee Airmen."

"My great-grandfather?"

"Yep. And you know what?"

"What?"

"He's very proud of you, too!"

I WOULD LIKE TO THANK . . .

My fantastic wife, J.J., who got to spend her summer vacation watching me do rewrites.

My dad, the late Thomas A. Grabenstein, who used to take us to Civil War battlefields in the 1960s and let my four brothers and me re-create entire battles in our heads.

My mom, who just happens to be my biggest fan.

My nephews Timothy John and Samuel Justus Grabenstein, for making sure their uncle's stories aren't boring.

My agent, Eric Myers.

Emily Pourciau, Lisa McClatchey, Nicole de las Heras, and everyone at Random House.

Sarah Abercrombie from Greenwich Country Day School in Connecticut, who showed me around their incredible campus.

The folks at JOE and Starbucks, who let me write in their coffee shops.

All the Morkal-Williamses, who not only give me great early reader critiques but also let me turn their names into characters in my books.

Rachel Curcio, Kate and Mary John, Nora Kaye,

Rodman John Myers, Riley Mack, Anna Bloomfield True, Jemma Glenn Wixson, and all the kids, students, teachers, and librarians who help me write these stories and then tell all their friends to read 'em.

Finally, Zipper would like to thank Fred, who helps me write the dog bits.

CHRIS GRABENSTEIN's first two books for younger readers, *The Crossroads* and *The Hanging Hill*, both won the Agatha Award, while *The Crossroads* also won the Anthony Award and received a starred review in *Booklist*.

Chris was born in Buffalo, New York, and moved to Chattanooga, Tennessee, when he was ten. After college, he moved to New York City with six suitcases and a typewriter to become an actor and writer. For five years, he did improvisational comedy in a Greenwich Village theater with some of the city's funniest performers, including this one guy named Bruce Willis. He used to write TV and radio commercials and has written for the Muppets.

Chris and his wife, J.J., live in New York City with three cats and a dog named Fred, who starred in *Chitty Chitty Bang Bang* on Broadway. You can visit Chris (and Fred) at chrisgrabenstein.com.

Don't miss Zack's next spooky
adventure in the
Haunted Mystery series:

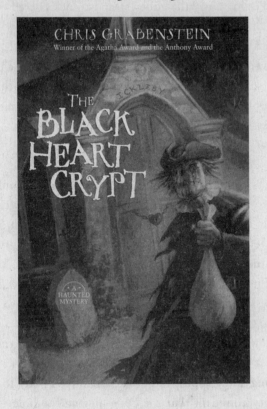

$Someone\ else$ was in the cemetery.

Zipper hunkered down on the ground in pounce mode.

Zack pressed his back against the Ickleby family crypt in an attempt to disappear into the shadows.

Sticky cobwebs attacked the back of his head, making him feel like he'd just brushed up against a giant wad of cotton candy. Peeling away the gooey strands, Zack peered over at a cluster of grime-streaked headstones, where he saw a burly man with a bushy beard, who was dressed in coveralls, sinking his shovel blade into the ground, digging up rocky clumps of dirt. A softly glowing lantern propped atop a nearby headstone projected his hulking shadow up into the tangled tree branches, where it loomed like a floating ogre.

Fortunately, the guy wasn't a ghost. Zack could tell. Ever since he'd moved to Connecticut from New York City with his dad and stepmom, he'd learned a whole bunch of junk about the spirit world—what ghosts can do and what they can't. He probably knew more than any eleven-year-old should legally be allowed to.

For instance, he knew that a ghost could take over the body of its blood relative, but unless it did that, it couldn't do much besides wail and moan and try to scare you into hurting yourself.

A ghost couldn't hold a shovel, and in Zack's experience, digging a hole in the ground by lantern light wasn't exactly something an evil spirit took over a relative's body to do. He felt pretty confident that the dude digging the hole wasn't a ghost or a possessed person.

The man started singing as he dug, a tune Zack recognized from recess on the playground:

*"Don't ever laugh when a hearse goes by,
  For you may be the next to die."*

Zack looked at Zipper and put a finger to his lips. They would try to tiptoe out of the graveyard without being seen or heard.

*"The worms crawl in, the worms crawl out,
  The worms play pinochle on your snout."*

Zack and Zipper crept closer to the gate. The man kept digging, kept up his steady *stomp-slice-shook-flump, stomp-slice-shook-flump.*

*"There's one little worm that's very shy,
  Crawls in your stomach and out your eye."*

Zack and Zipper made it to the graveyard gate.

The digging stopped.

"Isn't that right, boy?"

Okay. Zack didn't remember those lyrics. He pushed open the squeaky gate.

"Freeze!" the gravedigger shouted.

Zack froze.

And this time, Zipper obeyed, too!

Somewhere in the distance, Zack heard a stray cat meowing at the moon.

Then he heard boots clomping up behind him.

"I heard you callin' to your dog, boy," said the man, who kept coming closer. "Zipper. What kind of name is that for a dog?"

Slowly, Zack turned around.

The man was standing six feet behind him, holding his clay-draggled shovel like a knight's lance with one hand, the flickering lantern with the other.

"Well," said Zack, wishing his throat weren't so dry, "Zipper is very fast and . . ."

"Dogs ought to be named Fido, Duke, Sparky. What you two doin' here, anyway? Cemetery's closed."

"Um," said Zack, "Zipper chased a cat up the hill from the highway."

"A cat?" The creepy gravedigger raised the lantern up beside his craggy face. "You sure it weren't a dog? A big black dog?"

Zack gulped. "Pardon?"

The gravedigger bugged out his eyes. "A big black dog with fiery-red eyeballs. What some folks call a Black Shuck, a ghostly black beast what guards graveyards from foul spirits." The man grinned menacingly. "Wonder why he let you two in."

"It was just a cat," said Zack.

The stray cat yowled again. With its strangled cry, it sounded like a baby screaming for its bottle.

"Well, we better get going."

"Yep. You should. Ain't very wise to be in a boneyard this close to Halloween."

The gravedigger raised his shovel. "Git!"

"We're 'gitting,'" said Zack.

"Good! And don't never come back here no more!"

"Don't worry," said Zack. "We won't."

Because a graveyard was the last place Zack Jennings wanted to be.

Too many worm-eaten ghosts with pinochle cards up their snouts.